GermLine

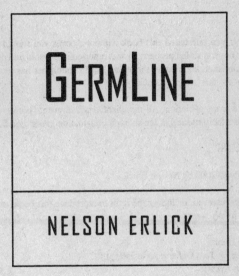

GermLine

NELSON ERLICK

A TOM DOHERTY ASSOCIATES BOOK
NEW YORK

This is a work of fiction. All the characters and events portrayed in this book are either products of the author's imagination or are used fictitiously.

GERMLINE

A Forge Book
Published by Tom Doherty Associates, LLC
175 Fifth Avenue
New York, NY 10010

www.tor.com

Forge® is a registered trademark of Tom Doherty Associates, LLC.

ISBN: 0-765-34031-3
Library of Congress Catalog Card Number: 2002034689

First Edition: January 2003
First mass market edition: November 2003

Printed in the United States of America

0 9 8 7 6 5 4 3 2 1

For Cheryl—
who always knew that I could,
and made it so

ACKNOWLEDGMENTS

My unending gratitude for *GermLine* extends in many directions:

To the physicians, scientists, ethicists, reporters, and undiscovered philosophers—sources of the hundreds of documents on which I constructed this work. If only humanity developed at a pace that rivaled its science.

To my editor, Natalia Aponte, who cultivated this work with her deft insights; to my assistant editor, Paul Stevens; to the many people in the copyediting, art, marketing, and sales departments at Tor Books; and to all Tom Doherty Associates who've supported me and worked tirelessly on my behalf.

To my agent, Susan Crawford, who happily nurtured this literary novice, who always had a word of encouragement, and who always made me feel special as she guided me through the heavily mined road to publication.

To my mother, Estelle, who made my education a priority even after my father died; to my children, Rayna and Melissa, who conscientiously respected the "Do Not Disturb" sign on my door; but most of all, to my wife, Cheryl, whose skillful editing of my barrage of drafts enabled this work to be born.

PART ONE

THE FIRST COMPONENT—YEAR 6 OF THE PLAN

1

Beneath the spinning laser lights, in the midst of his ball-room crammed with guests dancing to the band's charged Latin beat, E. Dixon Loring stared up at the bearer of disaster who walked along the mezzanine. The courier, in turn, located Loring, the party's host: a robust man, six feet two inches tall with perfect posture, a thick shock of black hair, and strong, wide, chiseled features. The courier's eyes never wandered from Loring. Slowly, the courier descended the grand staircase and skillfully slipped among guests meandering across the ballroom floor. As he approached Loring, he reached into his jacket pocket.

Not yet fifty, Loring had achieved success much earlier in life, and had long since perfected an aura of confidence, power. Those entering Loring's sphere felt compelled to gain a sliver of his grace. But never the courier. Loring gulped down his Dom Perignon.

The courier handed him an envelope.

"Have you seen the contents?" Loring asked.

The man's lips grew taut. "The envelope is sealed, sir."

Barely able to hear the courier's voice above the soiree's din, "Did he say anything?"

"He said that it was inadvisable to transmit the decrypted information by any means other than courier."

Loring tore open the envelope. Merlin had obviously cracked

Bergmann's personal files. If those files corroborated what—

"Sir, I'm sure he didn't intend for you to read it—here," the courier said, glancing at several guests, uncomfortably close.

Loring shot a scowl at the courier, then unfolded the envelope's contents. He scanned the document, picking up key phrases:

- ". . . we are not creating replacement tissue for grafts or breast reconstructions . . ." on the middle of page one;
- ". . . organic scaffolding will be used to make towers for the suspension bridge to Hell . . ." on the bottom of the page;
- ". . . I've read their Reconstruction Treatise. It details . . ." on page two;
- ". . . the SUE must be destroyed . . ." on page four;
- ". . . everything in ReGenerix Technologies must go. The horror must be stopped now, *before* it's born . . ." on page five;
- and finishing with ". . . Claire, I've left instructions for you and the children. You'll find them in the usual place. I have loved you, always. You've known, but I'm not sure the children do. When this is all over, tell them. Maybe they'll understand. Good-bye, Claire. God forgive me."

"Bergmann's cracked," Loring muttered.

"Sir, would you like to formulate a response to—"

"How long ago did you receive this?"

The man touched a button on his watch. "Two hours and forty-two—"

Loring shoved the courier from his path, briskly weaved through his guests, and charged up the grand staircase two steps at a time. At the mezzanine level, he whipped out his wireless, punched in "#1," and held it to his ear. He strode down a deserted hall to a private elevator.

"Yes, Mr. Loring?" a voice sounded over the receiver as the elevator doors shut.

"Merlin, where are you?" Loring asked.

"Research Triangle Park, North Carolina," the voice answered. "Did you get my—"

"Where's Bergmann?"

A pause. "We don't know. He's not at his house. We're en route to the facility now. ETA is ten minutes."

"Seal off ReGenerix Technologies."

"Already done."

"We may be too late." The elevator doors opened. Loring headed for the last room on the right. "Merlin, you read Bergmann's logs hours ago. Why didn't you stop him yourself?"

"It was your decision to make, not mine," the voice whispered. "And Bergmann is a pivotal element in the Plan."

Loring burst into his library at the end of the corridor. The door locked behind him. "After all these years, don't you know that I trust—"A wailing horn sounded from his receiver. "What's going on?"

After a moment, "Security breach at ReGenerix."

"Where?"

"Bio-scaffold Room. A team is on its way."

Loring hurried to the desk at the far end of the library and booted the computer system with inlaid keyboard on his desk. "Patching in to ReGenerix closed-circuit."

"Here, too," answered the man at the other end.

He sat back and waited for the projection screen on the far wall to activate. The ReGenerix Technologies Incorporated logo, a golden bird rising above a field of grain, filled the screen. After submitting to a retinal scan and voiceprint analysis of his password, the security camera view of the Bio-scaffold Room appeared on-screen. Six machines lay in view, each containing fine strands of polylactic acid polymer that emerged from copper-colored rods and wound onto densely wrapped spools. Beneath each machine lay stacks of micron-thin porous plates. Loring panned the surveillance camera past a central workstation to the remaining scaffolding. Within the seventh machine, a man in a white coat lay on his back, eyes open, chin snuggled impossibly between shoulder blades. "Merlin, is that—"

"We'll know in a moment," the man answered.

Loring watched four guards burst into the room. Guns drawn, three of them covered the fourth, who rushed to the man caught in the machine. Loring manipulated the security menu and spoke directly to them. "This is Mr. Loring. Is that Dr. Bergmann lying there?"

All guards turned toward the security camera in the corner opposite the machines. The nearest man answered, "Uh, no, sir."

"Then who the hell is it?"

"Dr. John Neuman, a project manager."

"Dead?"

"Very, sir. His neck's crushed. Not the sort of thing that could happen by acci—"

"Any sign of Bergmann?"

The guards looked around and shrugged. "Sir, we—"

Loring heard a distant bang. The camera shook. "What was that?"

"An explosion," Merlin answered in his ear. "It's in the Archive Room."

Bergmann—it had to be! The Archive Room contained project backup data. If Bergmann engineered a catastrophic loss of the mainframe data in Command and Control, and took out Main Lab, he would eradicate the two million man-hours of research behind Project MacDuff. "Merlin, were all project files downloaded to designated backup sites, off-campus? Or are all copies still in ReGenerix's mainframe?"

"I don't know. It will take some time to check," he answered.

"Get on it!" To the security personnel staring at the camera, "Bergmann will be heading for C and C. Get a team there, now!"

The lead guard depressed his communicator. After a static-filled exchange, "There already is a team there, sir."

"Great. Have them—"·

"Sir, they can't get in. The titanium doors have been sealed and pressurized."

"How long to breach it?"

The man sighed. "Twenty minutes."

"You'll have to do better than that!"

"Sir, even if we were under full-scale attack—"

"We *are* under full-scale attack! Blow them off if you have to!"

"Dixon, we've got another problem," Merlin's voice rang in his ears. "Someone's activated Protocol 1117—from inside C and C."

Loring crossed his arms. "Don't tell me. The override's been taken out."

"I'm sorry. There's nothing we can do. In ninety seconds, all Project MacDuff files will be irretrievably purged from Re-Generix's mainframe."

"Which means that we'll have to take Bergmann alive—"

"Unless we have a full backup set of project files off-site," Merlin finished. "I should know soon."

"You were right, old friend. I should have listened to you and had Bergmann removed at the first sign of trouble. You're due another big 'I told you so.' As usual."

"Do you smell something?" Loring heard one of the guards on-screen ask.

The four men in the Bio-scaffold Room lifted their heads and sniffed.

"Yeah, I do," one man answered. He crinkled his nose. "Bitter, like—"

"Nitric acid?" another finished.

Loring checked the screen. Behind the guard on the far right, at the base of one of the machine legs, was a small white disk. He zoomed in on the machine's base. As the site focused, it appeared to be two biscuits shaped like disks strapped to the machine's support struts by duct tape—with blasting caps and timers attached. "Get out of—"

The camera displayed static.

"What's happening, Merlin?" he yelled into his wireless.

"I've just entered the building. Bio-scaffold is gone. The mainframe has been purged. Bergmann is in Main Lab. And Dixon, whatever he has planned for the SUE and for himself, we will not get there in time."

Loring winced. "Without off-site copies, this will be a total loss. Six years!"

"Have faith. We are not there yet. Hold!"

"Merlin, what is it?"

No answer.

"Merlin?"

"There may yet be a chance. Dr. Bergmann in Main Lab would like to speak to you."

"Put him through!"

The screen displayed Main Lab: a sterile, white, three-hundred-foot-long chamber with a seven-story ceiling. Impregnated high in the back wall was the eighty-by-twenty-five-foot double-thick observation window from C&C. Main Lab proper, seemingly built to accommodate a battalion, was empty, except for a single, hastily constructed dais supporting a black cylinder on a bolted table. Freestanding poles, cameras, and monitors partially ringed the cylinder, all controlled from behind by a workstation. Dr. Wyndom Bergmann strode to center stage, his yellow biohazard suit muffling footsteps that echoed across the expanse. "Nice tux, Dixon. Leaving the party, or just arriving?"

"Wyndom, you said you were taking a month's vacation."

"No, *you* said I was taking a vacation." Bergmann laid his hand on the cylinder's gleaming black veneer and ran his fingers along its long axis. The SUE was precisely four feet long and utterly smooth, except for fiberoptic ports protruding from each side and flattened ends with hormonal- and nutrient-infusion pumps and excretion-sac outlets. The new modifications, specifically the infusion pumps and sonographic monitor for sequestered application or network integration, had not yet been installed. Bergmann ripped off the hood of his biohazard suit and exposed his ruddy face and thick blond hair. "You lied to me."

"I informed you, in writing, that we were pushing forward with the prototype."

"Initialize, yes, demonstrate, no! Tell me, Dixon, who did you invite to watch the beginning of the end of humanity?"

Loring pressed back into his chair and released a long sigh. "You're overwrought. I shouldn't have scheduled the demo without you. I allowed production pressures to override the human side of the equation. I know this was just once a dream in your mind. That the SUE is your handiwork."

"Classic E. Dixon Loring, charming to the end."

"I'll cancel the demo if that's what you want. But we are, after all, working for the betterment of man."

Bergmann checked on three disks planted at the base of the SUE and workstation. "I'm no longer gullible."

Loring zoomed the camera in on the disks. Each had blasting caps. "What are those?"

"RDX, the main ingredient in C4. Hexamine with nitric acid and acetone, baked with flour. Archives was first, then scaffolding. There's half a dozen planted here and in C and C."

"Wyndom, pull back from the edge. We can forget what's happened."

"Forget that I had to kill poor Neuman? Forget the four men who died when the scaffolding room went up?" Nearly in tears, "Forget the plague you plan to unleash on the world? Correction, the world you plan to create as a plague?"

"Your SUEs could save ten million ba—"

"I've seen your treatise!" Bergmann pointed at the black cylinder. "Look at the size of this place! Room enough for ten thousand Bokanovsky bottles!"

"The document was a capabilities treatise. Wyndom, don't throw your life away on a piece of fiction."

He banged on the SUE's fiberoptic port. "Without this, you can't complete your plan."

"I order—"

"You are no longer in a position to order people."

"I can take the lab by force."

"But not in time to take me alive." Bergmann turned away from the camera. He reached into a sack stashed behind the workstation, removed a biscuit, stuck a blasting cap in it, and held it out, gently. "And I cannot allow you to take me alive."

"Dixon, it's me," Merlin's voice sounded through Loring's wireless, still pressed tight against his ear.

"What have you got?"

"A complete set of project files at the San Francisco facility," Merlin declared.

Loring turned back to the screen with a subdued grin. "Wyndom, you don't want to die. Think of your family. That track-star son of yours at NC State. That brilliant daughter at NYU. And lovely, faithful Claire. What will become of them?"

"You'll never find them!"

"You're forcing me to—"

"I've destroyed all specs and data on Project MacDuff. In moments, this lab goes too. You've lost."

"Before you blow yourself and a quarter billion dollars into next week, you might want to reconsider." Loring leaned forward. "The information has already been disseminated."

Bergmann smiled. "Nice try. You never saw this coming."

"Three weeks ago, the Executive Gala. You were drunk, loud, more belligerent than usual. With that big mouth of yours you shot off 'Bokanovsky' one too many times." Loring sat back, grinning. "Wyndom, you're brilliant, but you're not the only one who reads classics."

"You're stalling!"

"Check it for yourself. All Project MacDuff files have been copied and stored safely beyond your reach."

Loring watched as Bergmann carefully placed the explosive on top of the SUE and took out a notebook computer. He punched in a series of commands. "It's true." After a long, shuddering exhale, "At least you don't have my soul."

"A soul? Life is just chemistry, which we can quantify and manipulate."

Bergmann grabbed a freestanding pole and smashed it against one of the Main Lab cameras, then against a monitor filled with Loring's smile. The monitor showered sparks, tipped, and crashed onto the floor. He spun around with the outstretched pole, striking each camera and monitor to a glittering symphony of orange-yellow sparks and glass shards.

Loring's screen went blank. Reestablishing contact with one of the security cameras in C&C, he directed the camera toward Main Lab, then zoomed in through the great window onto the lone dais with the black cylinder. "Destroying the lab accomplishes nothing. Another site will be up and running within months, probably weeks." Loring whispered, "Surrender the lab. Spare your family the grief."

Smoke filled C&C, obscuring Loring's view. The shadows of

three guards appeared through the haze. They trained their automatic weapons on Bergmann, visible on the lab floor far below the window.

"Wyndom, it doesn't have to end here."

"You're right, it doesn't." Bergmann, resigned, visibly shaking, picked up the RDX-impregnated biscuit sitting atop the SUE. "But hopefully, it will." He threw the explosive at the control room. It arced, long and loping toward the glass—and fell short of the wall. It disappeared from view.

A searing blue fireball erupted. The security camera stopped transmitting.

Loring turned off the screen, strutted to one of the library shelves behind him, and picked up his favorite novel. He skimmed it absently, fluttering through its pages, and lingered on the last paragraph while he listened to Merlin confirm what he already knew. Relieved, he closed the book.

PART **TWO**

THE SECOND COMPONENT—YEAR 7 OF THE PLAN

2

SATURDAY
Between Tiburon and Belvedere, California   2:31 P.M.

Kevin Kincaid, MD, PhD, took his foot off the accelerator, rolled down the window, and motioned the line of traffic behind him to pass. Sailboats, single-masts, crimson, white, topaz, and blue, bursting with wind, skirted across the brisk bay's shimmering water in a visual symphony. Beyond the corner of Tiburon peninsula, I-580 bisected the bay. He sucked in sweet brine air.

"We lost?" a sultry, sleepy voice behind him asked.

"Nope. We're heading north on Paradise Drive and," turning his 140,000-mile minivan to the right, "now on Antilles Way. We're a mile from the marina." He shifted in the driver's seat for the third time in half a mile. He'd already slid the seat back as far as it would go, trying to find some semi-comfortable position. Nothing helped.

"When are you going to take care of your problem?" asked his wife from the backseat.

Kevin Kincaid was a huge, overpowering man of Irish descent: six feet seven inches, with thick, rust-red hair, great green eyes, and freckles peppering his clean-shaven face. He could feel his wife scrutinizing his oversized belly. Too many hours spent with patients in the operating room or on the hospital floor had left him with too little time to care for himself. Between patients, he'd gobbled down anything starchy, or sweet, or that prolonged his stamina. Now, seventy-five pounds overweight, his belly hung far over his belt and chafed the steering wheel as he drove. His gray suit, the only one that fit, was frayed from being let out too many times. And with his meager stipend and two children and a wife to support, there wasn't enough money for a custom-tailored new one. But his legs remained thin and his puffy face had the still-handsome outline of a thin man trapped inside an obese body. "When I'm done the residency," he said. "Promise."

"I've heard that before," she said. "Why are we slowing down?"

Kevin gazed at his wife. "To take in the view." His photographic memory, along with his strong intellect, had helped him sail through medical school. Now, the peaceful image of his wife set against the beautiful harbor would be permanently seated in his mind—and always accessible.

Helen Kincaid, eyes closed, sat on the second-row bench between her sleeping children. Silken strands of mahogany hair cradled her face. Her delicate fingers stirred, her white gold wedding band sparkling in the afternoon sun. She opened her gray-green eyes, cocked her head, and smiled. "You're sweet." She tried to snuggle into her seat. "Kids are quiet."

Kevin glanced along the periphery of the rearview mirror. A toddler with curly brown locks slept in a child seat on one side of Helen while an infant in a seat restraint gurgled on the other side. "Looks like Jessica and Kathy are both out for the count."

"Twenty minutes of peace. If nothing else, I should thank your uncle for that."

"Helen, he is my only living relative."

"No, he's not!"

Yes, of course. Donny, Kevin thought. Without looking in the rearview mirror, he could feel her disapproval at his avoidance of his only brother.

"At least Donny's not bizarre."

"Uncle Dermot isn't bizarre. Eccentric, maybe."

"He once told me that when he stares hard at the horizon, he can see the back of his head. Kevin, don't place the future of this family in that man's hands."

"We haven't heard what he has to say."

Helen fiddled with her diamond and gold wedding ring. "I

don't have to. You're finishing your residency in two weeks. You've already accepted a great offer in Philadelphia with a chance to do first-class research. Then, your uncle, who's been just across the bay all these years, who you've only seen once, who's never seen your children, out of the blue calls you with an opportunity of a lifetime. Should I be suspicious?"

A glossy wood sign proclaiming "North Tiburon Marina" appeared on the right. Porsches and Mercedes lined the access road and filled the yacht club parking lot. A man, with an *L*-shaped scar on his temple, lay stretched out in his BMW convertible, soaking in sun and sea. Kevin turned his ancient green minivan onto Leeway Road and chugged up a winding, eucalyptus-lined drive. Cool, pungent air mixed with brine as they passed stone-arched gates lining the road. "These places start at three mil. Uncle Dermot might know more than you think."

Helen unbuckled her seat belt, leaned forward, and placed her hand on her husband's cheek. Kevin slowed down and pulled over to the side of the road. She swiveled his face toward her. "Kevin, promise me you won't make any commitment before we've discussed it."

"Helen, I—"

"Promise me!"

As he nodded, she drew his face into hers. Her lips met his, then parted. He appraised her trim, six-month-postpartum figure, and slowly smiled.

"Don't even think it," she said, returning his smile.

He grinned. "I wasn't."

"Of course you were. Everything's still tender, hon. I'll be back to normal in a few weeks." She patted his stomach. Excess pounds built from Coke, fried foods, and Baby Ruths wiggled. "And while we're on the subject, if I can lose my belly, you can lose yours. You've got to take care of yourself, family man. Physically *and* financially."

"I promise. No commitment till we talk."

They drove to a wrought-iron entrance with a sign marked "Kincaid," then up a manicured private road to a circular driveway by a house with floor-to-ceiling glass blocks joined at odd angles. An older woman with French-braided silver hair, long earrings, and Hawaiian print dress burst out of the glass foyer and charged at the car. Before Kevin could slam on the brakes, she'd pressed her face against one of the tinted side windows and was cooing at the baby.

"Good to see you, Aunt Chandra," Kevin said after getting out.

"Let me see those little ones!" Chandra squeaked.

Kevin unloaded the portable playpen, infant seat, diaper-laden knapsack, and toy bags while Helen gently placed the infant, Kathy, in Chandra's rocking arms. Kevin hoisted toddler Jessica on his hip. As he handed her off to Helen, he noticed a burly, solitary figure reminiscent of his long-dead father standing in the glass foyer.

"Your uncle's quite anxious to see you, Kevin," Chandra said.

"What about, Aunt Chandra?" Helen asked.

"Oh, something about 'leading the human race into the next era.'" She looked up at Helen. "Tea?"

The man lowered his binoculars and rubbed his face, irritating the scar on his temple. After seven hours in the BMW convertible parked in the marina, his back throbbed. He picked up the wireless phone and punched in a preset number. "It's Blount. Dr. Kincaid has a visitor. I checked the plate. Car's registered to his nephew, Kevin, a doctor at UCSF, Mount Zion, 'cross the bay."

"Is he alone?" a throaty voice asked.

"Didn't see anyone else. Didn't have a good vantage, though."

The voice on the phone hesitated. "For now, do nothing."

The living room was airy: a vaulted ceiling surrounded by glass walls overlooking a tiny English garden. Kathy gurgled happily between Helen and Aunt Chandra's arms as Jessica pushed a toy bubble machine across the carpet. Kevin sat stiffly on the couch and played with a loose thread dangling from his worn jacket pocket.

"Something to drink, lad?" Dermot Kincaid, PhD, asked, the residual brogue still strong, though he'd left County Cork as a child. Six-foot-five, thinning scalp of red hair, barrel chest and belly, the chief scientist at PolyPepGen, Inc. had a curriculum vitae of sixteen single-spaced pages.

"No, thank you. I'm still on call."

"Don't see each other much, do we?" Dermot stood, hands behind his back. "You remind me of your father, God rest his soul. But you're the spitting image of me when I was your age."

Kevin appraised Dermot's face and figure.

"Lookin' at yourself thirty years hence? Hmmh," rubbing his belly and laughing, "maybe less. Thought's not appealing, eh?"

Jessica picked up an old toy bucket filled with K'nex plastic construction pieces. "I'm sorry, Uncle Dermot," Helen said. "She's too young for pieces that size. She could choke on them."

Dermot bent over and traded the child a doll for the bucket. "They're not for the kids." He patted the toddler and grinned at Helen. "They're for your husband."

"Dermot, why don't you and Kevin go out to the patio and talk?" Chandra suggested.

The elder Kincaid tucked the bucket of play pieces under his arm. "I'll start the grill."

"Now, Dermot, you be careful. Last time you almost started a fire."

Kevin followed his uncle around a half-Olympic-sized indoor pool, then out to a tree-enclosed patio with an off-white chaise lounge, chairs, and table with matching umbrella. Dermot took a Dominican from a humidor on the table, ignited the propane grill, and lit his cigar on the hot rocks. After a few puffs, "What do you have lined up after your residency?"

"Something comfortable."

"Comfortable, eh? You signed papers?"

"Not till I pass the state boards."

"Good," blowing a smoke ring, "then you can work with me."

"For you?"

"No, lad. Not for me, *with* me."

"At PolyPepGen?"

"Nope."

Kevin plopped into the chaise lounge. "What'd you have in mind?"

Dermot unscrewed the top to the bucket and turned it upside down. Hundreds of plastic pieces clattered onto the glass table. Red, green, yellow, blue, purple. Half-inch rods with teeth; mini-ladders; clothespin-shaped pieces with four tendrils; half-starburst arrays with four sprouts ending in two receptors. A few pieces clanged on the brick patio. "Amino acids. Life's building blocks." Dermot picked through the pile of plastic for three small yellow, blue, and green rods. "Tiny, nonpolar amino acids like," pointing to each rod, "glycine, alanine, valine." He fished for purple and blue clothespin pieces. "Larger, charged and uncharged amino acids, like arginine, glutamine." Grabbing large yellow and green starburst arrays, "And very large amino acids, like proline, tryptophan."

Kevin repressed a smile: Uncle Dermot was an eighth-grade science teacher at heart.

"Only twenty different types of amino acids." Connecting the plastic pieces, "String a few together, you get an elementary polypeptide. String thirty or forty, you get a full-fledged protein." He held out the plastic chain, an unstable necklace of disjointed shapes. "Fifty thousand different proteins per cell, that we know of. My boy, proteins are the foundation of life. They form nerves, bones, organs, muscles, skin, hair. Without proteins, we're just bags of water. But," twisting the plastic necklace, "amino acids in proteins don't join like a chain. They fold, bend into beautiful, magnificent shapes: four-residue beta-hairpins, helix-turn-helix, beta-alpha-beta motifs, coiled-coil motifs. Now, for small polypeptides, like proteins of forty amino acids, you can somewhat predict how it'll fold. The three-D shape it'll take."

Kevin said, "Like the Dead End Elimination algorithm for

predicting protein structure that's based on a protein's minimum energy configuration."

Dermot nodded. "At least medical training hasn't completely stifled your academics, eh? But," sweeping all of the pieces on the table into Kevin's lap, "what if your protein had *thirty thousand* amino acids? What would it look like?"

"That's hard."

"Hard?" slapping his thigh. "A supercomputer using plausible rules for protein folding would require years to figure it out. Yet, the protein folds into its shape, instantly. Until we figure out how chains of amino acids fold into proteins, we'll always be a step behind Nature, looking up her ass, trying to decipher her proteins, instead of designing better ones ourselves."

"Nature's been designing proteins three billion years. We've been at it thirty. We've got a hell of a lot of catching up to do."

"Less than you might think, lad." He turned away, manipulating the plastic necklace. After a long, rich puff, "Kevin, I may not have been around, but I've been following your academic achievements since you were finger painting. You're too brilliant to be wasting your time cutting brains and spines."

"I'll also have an opportunity to do genetic research. Maybe work with vectors, very cutting-edge, maybe the key to solving genetic diseases. And remember, it's DNA that makes proteins."

"Uh-huh." Another long puff. "Even as a resident, I suppose you've had disappointments. Patients going sour. Incurable brain tumors. Spines mashed beyond repair. Must be frustrating. No matter what you do, a lot of your patients die, become vegetables, or cripples."

"I'm an MD first, a PhD second. I treat people first, study them second. I took an oath to give my patients the best I could—not a satisfaction-guaranteed warranty. Yeah, many of my patients will die or worse, no matter what I do, no matter how hard I try. I've learned to accept that. Every good doctor does. It goes with the territory."

"Doesn't have to, lad. Aren't you tired of cutting and sewing like a seamstress?"

Kevin stood. "Is that what they call brain surgeons these days?"

Dermot swiveled about and tossed the warped plastic shape into Kevin's lap. "I'm offering you the chance to design a brand-new nerve cell, one that transmits information twice as fast as existing nerves and is less prone to injury. You'll have top-notch neuroscientists, specialists in neurotransmitters and nerve synapse structures, at your call."

Kevin chuckled. "I've always enjoyed playing those computer evolution games. You know, the ones where they give you a planet or a city and let you build your own life-forms and civilizations. It's very satisfying to play God."

"This is not a game, lad. Try screwing your head into reality."

"C'mon, Uncle Dermot. Stop pulling my chain. The reality is that nobody can predict large protein structures, let alone design them!"

"It took mathematicians three hundred years to prove Fermat's Last Theorem." Rolling the cigar in his hand, "Child's play. I've developed a software package that *perfectly* simulates the environment of different cells. Considers water-attracting, hydrophilic, constraints. Water-repelling, hydrophobic. Thermodynamic. The presence of proteins and factors already existing in the cell."

"How does—"

"A physics-based computational approach, lad. Totally unique. My protein prediction software program uses multi-body interactions from an expansion of the free energy based on the molecular relative weight, as determined by Z-score optimization, conformational space annealing methodology, and multiple linear regression. This allows hierarchical *ab initio* prediction of a protein's structure. Even using a Q8 refined accuracy index—the standard's only a Q3—my program's *perfect*." Approaching Kevin, "My program's magnificent, fully compatible with every major protein database on the planet. You tell it what properties you want your protein to have, and it'll design it for you." Dermot put out the cigar on the glass table. "Kevin, I'm offering you a chance to be a partner in my new firm. To lead the human race into the next era. And become rich beyond dreams of avarice."

"Let me see the program."

"It's not safe to keep it here. I have it at PolyPepGen, under lock and key."

"You're a PolyPepGen employee. Isn't the program theirs?"

"*I* developed it! But they're burying it. No publicity. No credit. *My* breakthrough is as important as Watson and Crick's discovery of DNA. What I've accomplished warrants nothing less than a Nobel prize!"

If it exists, Kevin thought. He said, "But what can you do, legally?"

Dermot shook, his face reddening. "Reverse engineering. I've made a few personal changes in the program's specs. I'm calling in an independent software design team to create a new program from the ground up. In six months, I'll have my own program, free and clear. Then, Kevin, you and I can get down to serious work."

Kevin swallowed hard. The man was a genius, but it was impossible to distinguish reality from risky extrapolation. Kevin's father had always said that his younger brother had been touched. "Maybe we can talk in a year or—" His right jacket pocket beeped. "Excuse me." He took out a wireless phone. "Dr. Kincaid speaking." He nodded. "I understand. Right." Pause. "Uh-huh. I'll be there ASAP." And hung up. "Emergency at the hospital. I have to go back into the city."

"Kevin, what I'm offering you could be the way to fix poor Donny."

He wheeled around angrily. "Don't do that! Don't you ever do that!" He headed to the door. "I should be back in time for dinner."

Before the door slammed, he heard Dermot mutter, "Boy's got his priorities screwed up."

Anthony Blount swung his binoculars from bay to hillside, and waited until the minivan disappeared before reporting in by wireless. "The nephew just left. I got a better look this time. He was alone."

The voice on the phone asked, "Any activity in the house?"

"I saw Kincaid and the nephew talking in the back. And before you ask, I don't know what they said. You know the doc's too smart to let his house be bugged. And there's too many trees. I didn't have a direct line of sight, so I couldn't use a dish. What about the nephew?"

"He is not your concern."

"And Kincaid?"

The voice hesitated before answering: "Proceed."

7:02 P.M.

Kevin beeped the horn again. Half a mile from the marina, and traffic was still crawling. A thick cloud hung over the waterway—angry, black, acrid.

The emergency hadn't been. The trek back to San Francisco, a complete waste. The pain-relieving device he'd implanted into Mrs. Fitzroy's back had worked flawlessly. No infection, no cerebrospinal fluid leakage, no faulty electrodes, no broken lead wires—just normal, expected postoperative pain. A problem that could have been fixed by a simple phone call to increase the dose of her pain pills, instead of a two-and-a-half-hour trek through traffic.

The air tasted bitter, burned. His nose stung. Swirling beams of blue and red lights from police cars flashed in his eyes. The line of cars crawled forward on the slick road toward an armada of fire engines. Police waved on rubbernecked drivers. Firemen in full regalia manned the trucks and hoses. *Fire at the marina?* he wondered. He didn't see any fire there, despite the hoses trained on the yacht club. He looked in the other direction. Police cars blockaded Leeway Road. He gazed up.

The hillside was charred.

Kevin slammed on the brakes. He kicked open the car door, ran out into lumbering traffic, and charged the roadblock. Skirting around a screaming traffic cop, he headed past ash-laden trees that smelled like burned antiseptic. Fire engines, field communication units, elevating platform trucks, and rescue vehicles with weary firefighters were slowly descending the hill. He chugged past the first of the stone-arched gates. The private road beyond led through black matchsticks to rubble. Foul, choking air seared his starved lungs as he stumbled forward. The wrought-iron entrance—the sign that had marked "Kincaid"—was now black, brittle. Trees that had lined the roadway—gone. He bore down toward the circular driveway, never lifting his head from the road. Men shouted directions around him. Their words indecipherable, alien, detached. Except one, who yelled, "Bet it all started right here. Damn these propane grills!"

Kevin's head lifted against his will. Dermot's glass house looked as if it had been thrust into a blast furnace, then left to melt. Near what had been the pool lay two large black, zippered bags. Kevin put his hands to his giddy head as a man placed two tiny body bags beside the others.

Client:	Association to Cure Genetic Disabilities
Agency:	Hedges, Coates, and Jones
Title:	Germline Gene Therapy: There but for the Grace of God
Length:	60 seconds
Production Co.:	Ellison Michaels Productions, Inc.
Date:	November 8

The following commercial aired on all major broadcast and cable networks the evening of Sunday, January 19, and late night/early morning Monday, January 20:

[VIDEO]:   The camera zooms in on a montage of young children suffering from genetic diseases. Shots emphasize the children's disabilities, including facial and physical deformities. Montage of shots of children in hospital beds hooked up to heart monitors and ventilation machines. Final shot freeze-frames on sick child gazing forlornly at camera.

[AUDIO]:   Off-camera voiceover (VO) of Dr. Kevin Kincaid begins halfway through opening montage.

DR. KEVIN KINCAID (VO): There, but for the grace of God, goes my child. Cystic fibrosis, muscular dystrophy, neurofibromatosis, sickle cell disease, Tay-Sachs, retinoblastoma, fragile X syndrome, Lesch-Nyhan syndrome, Down syndrome. The list of genetic diseases that attack our children goes on and on. So many spend their lives in sickbeds. And die, so very young.

[VIDEO]:   Dissolve to Kincaid standing Rod Serling–style in front of full-size graphic of human chromosomes with hundreds of call-outs marking genetic diseases.

KINCAID (ON CAMERA [OC]): The cells of our bodies contain DNA, the blueprint of life. DNA, written on twenty-three pairs of strands, called chromosomes. These chromosomes contain more than 30,000 genes that make us who we are. And sometimes, seal our fate. Our DNA has millions of places for tiny, fateful errors. For genetic diseases.

[VIDEO]:   Dissolve background to graphics of genetic diseases.

KINCAID (OC): Genetic diseases that strike fear in a parent's heart. Genetic diseases that lay dormant, but haunt us in later years: Alzheimer's, Huntington's, breast cancer, ovarian cancer. There, but for the grace of God, goes you, or I.

[VIDEO]:   Dissolve to animation of DNA entering cell.

KINCAID (VO): But for the first time in human history, we *may* be able to cure these diseases. To rid humanity of them, forever. The way is called germline gene therapy. Its promise is unlimited. And over the next few nights, I'll give you a peek at that promise.

[VIDEO]:   Dissolve to opening montage.

KINCAID (VO): But there are those who fear this promise. Who have already banned it because of wild, unfounded misconceptions. This is not right.

[VIDEO]:   Freeze-frame on face of child dying in hospital.

KINCAID (VO): Phone, fax, or e-mail your U.S. senators and tell them to *support* House Bill 601, to lift the ban on germline gene therapy. Tell your senators that you want to give our children a chance!

[VIDEO]:   End Tag: Add supered letters to lower third of screen.
SUPPORT HOUSE BILL 601!
GIVE OUR CHILDREN A CHANCE!ᴿᴹ
Paid for by the Association to Cure Genetic Disabilities.
Hold image for five seconds. Fade to black.

3

Lance Morgan had waited motionless beneath a moonless, starry sky in the cold sand for the desert to again grow silent. The footfalls and voices were gone, leaving only the distant sounds of sea lapping against beach. He'd chosen his observation site well: prone against the wayward side of the high sand dune, just below its crest, he was hidden from both the sea and the village. He poked his head slightly over the dune crest and brought his night-vision binoculars to his eyes. The binocs transformed black night into a harsh, quasi-surrealistic green. Isla de Tiburon, an isolated, restricted wildlife sanctuary, peeked over the horizon. Before it, the seemingly tranquil waters of El Infiernillo strait hid their treachery: changing currents, shifting sandbars, shark schools. Each had nearly killed him before he made the mainland. And at the shoreline was the Seri village of El Desemboque, a handful of traditional domed huts of ocotillo sticks and tarp scattered between metal-roofed concrete dwellings. He checked the estimated two miles of desert stretching between his position and the village. Nothing moved among the giant saguaro cactuses marching to the sea.

Tall, ungainly, emaciated, Lance had four days' growth on his face. Stringy blond hair fell about his shoulders. He wore a ripped flannel shirt and a belt with a big silver and turquoise buckle that held up well-worn jeans that matched the pale blue of his eyes. Shivering in the cold night air, he pulled out a pocket recorder and whispered, "Tracy, I made it off Tiburon Island. Was damn lucky. Right now, it's after two A.M. and I'm looking out over the main Seri village. You'll have to settle for audio. The camera doesn't record in pitch dark." He rubbed his frosty fingers. "I can't let the video I shot affect me. It's graphic, but it's not enough. I've got to *prove* that Tiburon is real. Show what the Collaborate's planned for us all. And I'm telling you, Sis, it's worse than Dad imagined. Much worse."

Lance clicked off the recorder and scanned the village. Two patrol boats pulled alongside a rickety dock. Twenty Seri men with long dark hair and dressed in jeans and long-sleeve shirts assembled on the beach. The boats quickly docked. Mexican soldiers disembarked, their semiautomatic rifles poised. Searchlights drenched the beach, burning out chunks of Lance's night vision. One boat lowered a black, zippered bag onto the dock. One of thirty burly soldiers hoisted it onto his shoulders. Weapons drawn, the unit advanced on the villagers.

After centuries of slaughter by Spanish conquerors, European colonists, and provisional governments, in the 1960s, the Mexican government had expatriated the entire Seri tribe, the last few hundred, from their native Tiburon. They'd moved the nation onto the desert mainland in prefabricated cement bunkers and made them totally dependent on daily deliveries of water trucks. Now they belonged to the Collaborate.

Lance refocused the binocs. A soldier gesticulated heatedly to four Seris. The marine contingent slowly swung their rifles toward the tribesmen. The Seri elders locked arms. An officer pointed to two soldiers. Both fired their rifles. Sand sputtered behind the Seris, but the tribesmen did not waver. The clipped *pop* sounds reached Lance seconds later.

The officer pointed at a Seri elder with shoulder-length hair in the middle of the human chain, then directed four rifle barrels at the tribesman. He waited, shrugged. With a flick of his wrist, the elder Seri collapsed, dead before the sounds of rifles reached Lance. The Seris scattered. With their searchlights and weapons and black sack, the soldiers marched into the desert on the far side of the village.

Lance slammed his fist into the sand, then whispered into his pocket recorder, "Mexican troops just showed up at the village carrying a body bag. Killed a tribesman. I think the troopers have a specific place they want the body buried, regardless of tribal custom. Tracy, we need something to corroborate the tape. I'm going to see where the troopers bury the body." The soldiers were passing beyond view. He gathered his equipment, placed it in a knapsack, and added, "Sis, whatever you do, don't share any of this with the others!"

West River Drive
Philadelphia, Pennsylvania   *4:33 A.M.* **(EST)**

Drenched in sweat, steam rising from sneakers, Dr. Kevin Kincaid ran relentlessly in the early morning cold. Street lamps reflecting off the sluggish Schuylkill River eerily illuminated the runners' path on Philadelphia's West River Drive. Breath condensing into icy fog capsules, legs churning against frozen asphalt, Kevin dug deeper into himself to hasten the arrival of the second wind. The path led beneath 170-foot-high concrete supports for the twin bridges overhead, and the 100,000 cars daily traversing the river. Time to head back.

Kevin returned along the winding river path. Four miles to Boat House Row, a string of century-old rowing clubs that, outlined in soft white lights, glowed like gingerbread houses. Six miles to the hospital. A perfect running day: no ice on the ground; the air too cold for muggers. When would his second wind, and its release, come?

Though his hair was trimmed short and he'd grown a mustache, both peppered with errant gray hairs, Kevin retained the same handsome, facial features he'd had before Tiburon. But his belly, his bulk, were gone. He was very lean, thirty pounds underweight, but powerful-looking with broad shoulders and thick, muscular legs and arms. He exuded energy and vigor, but there was a worn quality just beneath the surface. And Kevin's eyes seemed darker, much darker, than during his days as a resident. Over the past ten years, running had become more than exercise that had shed his excess pounds, as Helen had wished.

He used running to reinvigorate his mind—a fleeting mechanism to counter the agonizing accuracy of his photographic memory constantly replaying the day he lost his family: the reek of charred flesh, the sight of body bags, the shock and horror of realizing what had happened. Each foot strike propelling him off the ground brought him closer to that treasured moment of release when the flute that had played "Amazing Grace" at the triple funeral stopped playing in his head.

The triple funeral, three caskets: two with the horrifically charred remains of his children; the third, empty. They'd never found Helen. Most of the Marin County officials had said that while they generally recovered all of the bodies following a fire, on occasion, one might remain missing. Perhaps she was lodged under a piece of bulldozed foundation, or buried under debris, or so badly destroyed by fire that nothing remained but a few errant bones. He'd almost accepted that he would never find his wife—until he learned months later that the lead investigator of the tragedy had not only refused to close the case, but had been examining Helen's background, and even had the gall to question her friends, as if she were responsible for the fire. Ten years later, the case was still open.

Kevin passed beneath the stone arch of an old trestle crossing the river. The parkland between river and jogging path widened, exposing an antique water-pumping station. Three miles to the hospital. *Purge the body, purge the mind.* That aphorism had built his physique, increased his stamina, honed his surgical skill, and vaulted him to national prominence in genetic research.

The release came. He smiled and closed his eyes as endorphins flooded his mind with luxurious, euphoric warmth. The funeral's haunting flute fell silent.

Kevin opened his eyes. A runner had appeared forty yards down the path, heading in the same direction. Strange seeing a woman running alone, here, this time of day, of year. The runner's hair, silken, almost mahogany like Helen's, fell freely down her back and bobbed across her sleek running suit with each heel impact. He closed the gap. In the pale yellow light, her running suit looked amber. He remembered once, against his wishes, Helen had run at night. The street lamps had turned her blue suit to orange, the yellow strip running from the left calf to right shoulder, white.

The jogger ran directly beneath another street lamp. A white strip appeared on her suit.

"Helen?"

The woman turned toward him. It looked so much like Helen's face. She turned away and ran harder. He shook his head an instant—it couldn't be.

Kevin drew closer, almost bumping her. He stared at her profile as she tried to ignore him. They passed beneath a street lamp. She glanced momentarily at him. It *was* Helen's face, Helen's hair. And she had gray-green eyes—Helen's unique shade. Kevin felt his arms reach out to grab her.

She quickly pulled away, dashed across the road, ducked beneath an overpass, and disappeared.

Kevin lost his footing and tumbled into the road. Headlights bore down on him. He slipped and fell. The approaching horn blared. He rolled onto the curb just as a two-toned Chevy van swerved away. Cold, turbulent air blasted him. Slowly, he stood, one hand pressed against his throbbing right knee, and gazed at the gateway beneath the overpass.

Seri Reservation, Sonora, Mexico

Lance surveyed the site again: there was nothing but open desert. The soldiers had marched back to the village two miles south-southwest. He nervously approached the site.

The ground had no signs, no fences—just half-buried, haphazardly laid sandstone markers with corrosion-resistant numbers. He stepped carefully between the markers, partly in deference to the dead, partly in wariness of hidden trip wires. The Collaborate and their federal flunkies obviously wanted these graves kept secret, but why did they bury the bodies at all? Why not cremate them, destroy the evidence? *Because they might need a sample*, Lance thought, *like me*.

Marker 43 lay on a freshly patted mound. He knelt, pulled a hand spade from his backpack, whispered a prayer, then dug into sand. Working quickly, he cleared away a fist-sized hole before striking a vinyl bag in the shallow grave. He brushed away sand, exposed the bag, and pulled the zipper down. Cold flesh touched the back of his hand.

He recoiled. *You have to do this!* He shone his flashlight into the bag.

She was, perhaps, four years old, with dark skin with black braided hair, thin, desiccated lips, and dull, gelled eyes. The rest of the face was bloated, distorted.

Had this little girl ever been happy? Was she even capable of it? No, that was bigoted, a question her jailers would have asked. "Forgive me," he said as he took out a four-inch hunting knife and two vials of clear fluid. He cut a half-inch square in her left shoulder, peeled away the skin, freed up the piece of muscle, and placed the sample in a vial. The pungent odor of formaldehyde pounded his sinuses. He sealed the vial, scribbled on its label, and repeated the procedure on the other shoulder. "Tracy, I've got two samples from the girl I saw on the island," he whispered into the pocket recorder. His eyes watered as he zipped up the body bag, covered it with sand, and patted the surface smooth. He offered a moment of silence.

Voices from the direction of the village approached. Lance glanced at a swirling rose sky. Sunrise, soon. Villagers, outpost guards, or marines, it didn't matter. If they found him, they'd kill him, and the Collaborate would win. That frightened him more than dying. His jeep lay hidden behind a mound three miles south of El Desemboque, but the approaching soldiers blocked his path. He gazed to the north: nothing but sterile Sonoran desert hills. Lance gathered his equipment, and headed into the desert. His canteen was almost empty.

Select Procedures Wing
Benjamin Franklin Medical Center (BFMC)
Philadelphia   *9:15 A.M.*

Dr. Kevin Kincaid scrubbed furiously. Up, down: fifteen strokes per surface, four per finger. Sienna suds plopped into the basin and dissolved in water streaming out the spigot. Beneath the lather, the surgical brush's plastic bristles tore flesh. *Get a grip, Kevin! It wasn't her!* he thought. Systematically, he scrubbed his right wrist and up his forearm as he stared at the featureless wall of the clean room. *Purge the body, purge the mind.*

"Dr. Kincaid, everything all right?"

Kevin looked back over his shoulder at a stout woman in blue scrubs. "Fine, Becky," his surgical mask muffling his reply. Directing his eyes up, "Would you mind?"

She adjusted his surgical cap. "Nothing's too good for our TV star. Think I got a future as a Hollywood hairdresser?"

"Don't hitch your wagon to me. They're just commercials, and only running one week." He glanced down the hall. Holding out wet forearms, he headed toward the operating room.

The OR gleamed, a large chamber that combined a standard surgical suite with high-profile, innovative radiographic and diagnostic equipment. The patient lay on the table, draped in blue, his head shaved. Kevin's team, which included several surgical fellows, scrubbed and unscrubbed free-floating nurses, a magnetic resonance imaging technician, and an anesthesiologist, stood inside a giant metal drum shaped like a wine cask. The hollow drum formed an open-configuration magnetic resonance imaging system, or MRI, enabling the surgeon to peer deep inside the patient's brain, navigate safely past undamaged critical structures, and hone in on life-threatening tumors. Without the open MRI that guided the surgeon's hands and instruments through the brain in real time, the slightest misstep could leave the patient dead, or worse. One laser for digital scanning and two for tissue cutting/desiccation were implanted in the exterior walls outside the MRI magnetic drum. The ungowned tech manned a computer workstation that received and interpreted data, and instantly updated MRI images of the patient's brain on monitors flanking the table. Video cameras covered the room from every angle. Kevin checked the surgical instruments neatly laid on the stand, and the drill beside the tray. The nurse handed him a towel, then gowned him. He thrust his hands into latex gloves that snapped skintight.

"Got a gimp there, Kevin," the anesthesiologist said. "Putting in too many miles?"

"Just a scraped knee, Bransom."

"Try swimming, Nature's most perfect exercise. You can't fall."

"What, and come out looking like a prune?"

"Beats looking like a stick."

Kevin grinned at the anesthesiologist, then returned his attention to the patient. Because of his height, he had to duck his head and crouch forward inside the drum to avoid blocking part of the imaging system. Performing surgery for hours while stooped over often left him with a sore back that required periodic trips to the chiropractor. He gazed down at the shaven head of the man lying anesthetized on the table as a nurse raised the table. "How's my patient?"

"Doing fine," Dr. Bransom stated.

"Everyone, I hope you've got big smiles under your masks, 'cause today you're on camera," Kevin said to the team. Calling to the video engineer in the master control room via the intercom system, "Ed, we all set to record?"

A deep voice answered from the loudspeaker, "Standing by."

Kevin said to the surgical team within the magnetic drum, "The procedure we're taping today is going to the National Institutes of Health, and is also going to be used as a supplement for Continuing Medical Education credits in neurosurgery. The public relations people are also itching to get their hands on it, probably to cut some promotional pieces for the center here. So we'd all better watch our language. And there's one word that we absolutely, positively must not use."

"All right, I'll bite," Bransom said. "What word is that?"

"Oops!"

The loudspeaker voice said, "Five, four, three, two, one. You're on, doc."

Kevin looked directly at a camera. "I'm Dr. Kevin Kincaid. This videotape serves to document Benjamin Franklin Medical Center's ongoing commitment to excellence and research. Today's procedures are in conjunction with human gene therapy protocol number 1103-112 as designated by the National Institutes of Health, Office of Recombinant DNA Research, and have been reviewed and approved by the FDA." He introduced his surgical team, then said, "The surgical suite here in BFMC's Select Procedures Wing has been certified to meet NIH guidelines for biosafety of research involving recombinant DNA molecules, as described in Appendices G-2A and I-1A for physical and biological containment of host-vector systems."

He glanced down at the man lying on the table. "We will refer to this gentleman as 'Patient 24,' a 46-year-old white male with a Grade IV astrocytoma on the left temporal lobe of his brain. The tumor has proven resistant to surgery, chemotherapy, and radiation therapy. The prognosis for survival is three to six months." His mind started replaying the morning run—the image of Helen speeding out of sight. "This morning, we're going to fight Patient 24's battle on two fronts. First, we'll identify, isolate, and excise the tumor that grew back in the patient's brain since his last treatment. And second, using somatic gene therapy, we'll try to destroy the remnants of that tumor without damaging surrounding brain tissue. We'll do that by injecting special genes into the site. These genes are HSV-TK, short for herpes simplex virus thymidine kinase gene, and MDES, short for multiple drug-enhanced-susceptibility gene. Both genes will hopefully incorporate only in tumor cells, making these cells especially susceptible to the drug, ganciclovir, which we'll inject into the patient several days from now. This should kill the remaining tumor cells without harming surrounding brain tissue."

His knee brushed against the table. The irritation reminded him of the morning run, of Helen lost. He continued, "Now the biggest problem in gene therapy to date has been finding a way to efficiently get genes into cells. We do that by stuffing these genes into packages that can penetrate cells. We call these packages *vectors*. Vectors are the key component in gene therapy. One could have the most perfect gene in the world that could fix any genetic problem, but without a vector to insert it into the nucleus of a damaged cell, that gene is useless. It's like a young lady dressed for the prom, but without a ride." Gazing back at the camera, "BFMC's contribution has been the development of a unique vector named BFV.Syn108." Turning from the camera, "Diminish ambient lights to one-quarter, then initiate laser scan."

A laser activated. Thin red streaks appeared on the patient's shaved head. Each streak represented an anatomical structure lying deep within the skull. A projected green blob abruptly appeared on the patient's right temple. Kevin touched it with a pointer and checked the MRI-monitor screen just outside the drum. "That's our target. Mark the time: 09:31."

As Kevin stared at the green light on the patient's head, a surgical nurse placed a handle and blade between his thumb and index finger. Kevin ran the knife across the patient's scalp. A streak of blood followed. An assistant patted the site with a sponge, then retracted the skin edges, exposing bone. Another nurse handed him a drill with a tiny metal ball bit resembling a melon scoop. He revved the drill, then applied it to the skull. Chips of bone dissolved in a stream of sterile saline as he gently sculpted a perfect circle one centimeter in diameter. Resilient tissue appeared at the base of the tiny well. "We're now at the dura, the envelope surrounding the—"

"Amy, I told you last week to make certain that all of Dr. Kincaid's project records were ready for today's visit," said Joan Tetlow, the Senior Administrator of the Benjamin Franklin Medical Center. As always, she wore her hair tightly curled to hide the thinning from premature baldness that had plagued her since her late thirties and a conservative suit, selected from her narrow preference range of plum to amethyst and cut so as to minimize her pear-shaped figure.

"Ms. Tetlow, you told me to give the year-end reports top priority," her assistant, Amy, said. "Every one of BFMC's general ledger files, earnings and losses, quarterly reports, payables, accounts receivables, inventories, budget projections, all on your desk by nine this morning. Well, it was. And it took me and the accounting department the entire weekend to do it."

"Dr. Kincaid's project files were top priority, too."

"But when everything's top priority, nothing is," Amy muttered to herself.

"You want to move up in this world, Amy? Learn to anticipate." She scoured the bustling hospital lobby, but there was no sign of the VIP.

"Is there anything else, Ms. Tetlow?"

"No, you've done quite enough. You can go."

As Amy headed for the elevators, Tetlow quickly checked herself in a lobby mirror. Her suit and signature floral silk scarf draped around her neck and shoulders were perfect, offsetting the hatchet jaw she'd inherited from her father and had learned early in life would keep the boys away. Who needed them anyway? She was Senior Administrator of a major hospital; most of the boys in her high school class were probably still working on assembly lines. She declared herself presentable for the President of the Benjamin Franklin Healthcare Network, while trying not to think about her failure to update Kincaid's files. She knew the meeting would be unpleasant, at best. But she had survived the feeding frenzy of mergers, consolidations, selloffs, and layoffs. She had survived, thrived through the early, volatile days of the Benjamin Franklin Healthcare Network, revived this once-dead hospital on Lombard Street, and turned it into BFHN's flagship medical center. Ten years ago, she had recruited an unproven Kevin Kincaid to direct the new Department of Molecular Genetics and Engineering, a move that had proved wildly successful and eventually used to maneuver her own ascent to BFMC's Senior Administrator, and had firmly held the post for years—not bad for an RN-program washout. Yes, the president would be pissed, but as always, she would think of something to mollify him. She grabbed the arm of a brawny guard passing through the lobby. "Have you seen Mr. Grayson?"

"No, ma'am," the guard replied.

Tetlow headed toward the elevators. "I'll kill that driver if he took the expressway again." She respected Frederick Grayson: as President of the Benjamin Franklin Healthcare Network, he controlled an integrated healthcare system of twelve hospitals,

150 community medical practices, and 2,300 doctor-providers servicing close to a million consumer members. The only president BFHN ever had, Grayson had deep ties, unusual ties, to Mr. Loring, the CEO, who, according to several reliable sources, had a strange nickname for him.

A white limousine pulled up to the entrance.

She hurried through the main lobby. Wide glass doors parted for her. Her breath condensed in the cold as she waited beneath the marquee. Frederick Grayson stepped out of the limousine. He was trim, wore narrow, round, black-rimmed glasses, and had slicked-down, thinning red-brown hair—very Ronald Reaganesque with surprisingly little gray for a man in his mid-seventies. He also had severe scoliosis, a hump in his back due to a prominent curvature of the spine. He used a cane as he shuffled forward—which the doctors called an 'ataxic gait'—and always made certain that he kept his center of gravity directly over his feet. His cane wasn't constructed from the usual metal alloy, nor did it have the traditional curved handle. It was rattan, like a multifired stick used by martial artists, and had a bulbous end with two intricately carved birds: a dove and a falcon. At times, the cane made the man seem wise, almost grandfatherly; other times, it made him seem more like the aged emperor from *Star Wars*. He greeted Tetlow with a single, formal shake. Cane in hand, he slowly made his way across his lobby.

"Staying long in Philadelphia, Mr. Grayson?" asked Tetlow, respectfully trailing him.

"A few hours. I've business in the District tomorrow," Grayson whispered in his gravelly voice over his shoulder. "But I'll be back on Wednesday night. Mr. Loring is throwing a soiree at one of his residences to which you are invited. Now, I'd like to chat with Dr. Kincaid."

"He's finishing up in surgery, but he'll be done in time for the news conference."

"He is prepared?"

"Completely. With his intellect and that eidetic memory of his, he'll dance rings around the media. He'll provide them with a great story."

Grayson stopped in front of the elevators, slowly removed his glasses, and huffed hot air onto the lenses. "Ever noticed a certain dichotomy in the word *story*?" Wiping his glasses with a cloth from his jacket pocket, "A story can be a child's fable or a Pulitzer prize expose. Truth and deceit, described by the same word."

"The only story here is House Bill 601."

Grayson delivered a white-lipped smile. "Actually, there're three stories. First, the controversy behind the House of Representatives Bill 601 and its implications. Second, the Association to Cure Genetic Disabilities, of which BFHN is a prominent member, and the $300 million media blitz it launched this past week in support of HR 601. Culminating in a two–minute commercial during this Sunday's Super Bowl. And third, Kincaid himself, a leading researcher thrust overnight into the spotlight as the Association's spokesman, appearing nightly on all the major broadcast and cable networks." Grayson cupped his hands around his cane and pointed both index fingers at Tetlow. "The media has its inside-the-Beltway correspondents for politics, its financial correspondents to investigate the Association, and its science correspondents to explain the medical ramifications. But what the media doesn't have is a good grasp of Kincaid himself. That, Tetlow, is why the press is here. Now, how's he bearing up?"

"He doesn't care for the publicity, but accepts it because he knows it'll help funding."

Grayson pressed the *up* button. "I'd intended to inspect Kincaid's primary project files after chatting with him, but since he's tied up, perhaps now would be a good time to—"

"Why don't we go to the observation suite? It's equipped with closed-circuit monitoring, so you could talk to him while he's operating."

"Let's go straight to the files." Grayson noticed her pursed lips. "But then we can't, because they're not in order, are they?"

She hesitated. "They will be."

"I see." The elevator doors parted. "Then, the observation room it is."

The room looked like a hotel suite with rows of TV monitors. Tetlow flicked one on as Grayson sat on a brown leather couch. Dr. Kincaid appeared, center screen, holding a long, slender syringe, penetrating the patient's skull as he checked the needle's plotted position on an MRI-monitor. "He's injecting the vector complex now," she said. "He's almost finished."

Grayson leaned forward. "That's not the new vector, is it?"

"Absolutely not. That's BFV.Syn108. High-profile, NIH-approved. Been quite successful, too. Thirteen of fifteen patients followed have survived at least a year, which is remarkable considering that normal survival time is four to six months."

"Have him play that up for the press."

She nodded. "I'll make a note of it."

"What parameters have you set for disclosure at the press conference?"

"He's permitted to announce that he's currently working on a series of innovative vectors that may be ready for testing soon. He can tantalize the audience with a few of their properties, primarily vector efficiency and DNA-payload size. He's welcome to speculate how these new vectors will revolutionize gene therapy, and is, of course, encouraged to make the transition into the importance of HR 601." She adjusted her scarf. "But, he knows not to comment on any specifics, structure, or synthesis of the new vector class, because BFHN considers that strictly proprietary."

"How close is he to completion?"

"He's just waiting to dot the i's and cross the t's."

"If his organization skills weren't so poor, we'd know now," Grayson said. "How well will he perform?"

"He's convincing in the ads. Even better one-on-one."

"That's not what I asked."

She glanced at the screen, at Grayson, at the screen and back. "He's brilliant, dedicated, arguably the best in his field. When he puts his passion into his work, his excitement is contagious. If he stays focused, he'll wow them."

"In truth, you're wondering why we chose him as the Association's spokesman instead of hiring an actor?"

She smiled. "Probably because of the very qualities I just listed."

A corner of his mouth upturned. "Yes. That and circumstance."

Tetlow nodded and checked the speaker. "Mr. Grayson, they've stopped recording. You can now talk directly to him."

He nodded. Projecting his voice, "Dr. Kincaid. Frederick Grayson here."

On the monitor, Kevin glanced up from the surgical table, then resumed the procedure. "Good morning."

"What do you have to say for our new $30 million OR?"

Without looking up, "Why, thank you."

The surgical team exploded in laughter.

"Mr. Grayson would like to talk," Tetlow called out. "ASAP in the cafeteria."

"Okay, Joan. We're far enough along. My senior fellow can close." Stepping away from the table, Kevin mock-whispered, "You watch. After that crack, they'll bill me for the room!"

Still in surgical scrubs, Kevin descended the open-air staircase from the lobby to the cafeteria filling quickly with the lunch crowd. Weaving his way through diners carrying trays, he found Grayson and Tetlow sitting at a table and sat next to BFHN's president, who was eating a bowl of minestrone. Kevin looked up at the lobby overhead that ringed the dining area.

"Want some soup?" Grayson asked. "It's surprisingly tolerable."

"No thanks. The news conference is in ninety minutes," Kevin said, scanning the crowd.

"You look nervous," Grayson said between spoonfuls.

"I've lectured more times than I can count."

"It's not a lecture. Think of it as talking to sixth graders . . ."

Jessica would have been in sixth grade, Kevin thought, struggling against the image of her charred body, presented in perfect clarity by his photographic mind. The reek from burned flesh filled his nostrils.

". . . unruly, undisciplined, often hostile, they instinctively smell weakness . . ."

What do they teach in sixth grade these days?

". . . could ask you something completely unrelated . . ."

She had her mother's face. If she'd had her mother's intelligence . . .

"We'll be there to back you up, if you need us," Tetlow said. "But you won't."

Grayson handed him a sealed envelope. "This is for you."

Kevin opened it:

MR. E. D. LORING REQUESTS THE PLEASURE OF YOUR
ATTENDANCE WITH A GUEST AT HIS RESIDENCE ON
WEDNESDAY, JANUARY 22, AT 7 P.M., SHARP.
BLACK TIE. DIRECTIONS ENCLOSED.

"Naturally, you'll be attending," Tetlow said.

"I can arrange a limousine to pick up you and your guest," Grayson said.

"Don't bother," Kevin said. "I'll be coming alone."

"That can be remedied."

"Very kind, but—" Kevin stood, tipping over his chair. His eyes fixed on a spot in the lobby overhead.

"Dr. Kincaid, is something wrong?"

She strode by the railing overhead. Her hair, silken mahogany, cascaded over her back and draped her petite frame. The woman glanced absently at a mural on the dining area wall. Kevin honed in on her eyes.

"What? What is it?" Tetlow asked.

The woman turned to her right. Disappeared from view.

Kevin leaped over his chair and glanced against a resident in scrubs, who careened into a pair of social workers carrying trays. Salad and pie flew across a nearby table. Shoulders turned, he blew through the crowd, his large frame like a bulldozer, knocking patrons left, right. Indignant squeals and curses followed him. At the steps, he waved his arms, parting the crowd, and bullied his way up the final few steps. Standing at the top, fists clenched, he scanned the lobby: the circular main desk, the elevator banks, the gift shop, the chapel entrance, the reception areas. Nothing—no sign of her.

Tetlow stumbled up beside him.

"She was right here!"

"Who?" Grayson asked, hobbling up the last step.

"Helen. My wife. It was her. At least, I thought—it sure looked like her."

The BFHN president shrugged, then patted the surgeon's shoulder. "So many people pass through here every day, you almost might expect to see someone who looks familiar. Don't concern yourself. Ms. Tetlow will accompany you back to your office and ready you for the conference." To Tetlow, "When you're done, stop back at your office before you head to the auditorium together."

"I—I'm sorry. That was really—" Kevin hesitated. "I'm fine now. Fine."

Sonoran Desert

Lance squinted. The harsh morning sun peeked over another scrub-and-cactus-covered mound of rock sticking out of the desert floor. Surely this had to be the place. He scrambled up the slope, his empty canteen jangling on his hip. His planned escape route had been simple: circle southeasterly away from the village, then head south toward the jeep, hidden safely between two rock mounds. But somewhere along the trek, he'd become confused. Twice he'd trudged into mini-valleys where he'd sworn he had parked his jeep—and found nothing.

He slipped and scraped his knee raw on a jagged stone. His blue eyes had grown increasingly sensitive to the radiant sun. If the jeep wasn't over this peak, then either he was lost and had a sixty-mile trek south through the desert, on foot, without water, to Hermosillo—or they had found it. He caught his breath, stood, then assaulted the summit, shimmying through rocks and loose dirt up the slope. Groping the final fifty yards with cracked palms and shredding fingernails, he peered over the summit.

Across the ravine, tucked into the shadow of a giant saguaro cactus at the foot of a mound, sat the black jeep and the empty trailer he'd used to haul his powerboat. "Thank God." Lance charged down the hill, as if fighting knee-high drifts of snow. The hill tugged him down. He stumbled, face-first, onto the desert floor. Sand splattered against his tongue. He tried to spit out swarms of grain burrowed tight between his cheek and gums as he lifted his head. Staggering across the valley, he lunged into the delicious shade protecting the black jeep. He pulled out a plastic gallon of water sheathed in cool sweat from beneath the passenger seat, and greedily drank, washing away the desert in his mouth. Satiated, he looked back at the ravine. Heat waves arose from the desert floor, distorting the distance, though it was not yet noon in the coolest season of the year.

This hidden dry valley seemed unfamiliar. Only thirty-six hours ago, he'd parked the jeep between desert foothills after having dumped his powerboat south of El Desemboque—the powerboat that had sunk in the treacherous strait and forced him to make a desperate escape from Isla de Tiburon aboard an abandoned Seri reed boat. Something about this valley should have seemed familiar. Nothing was. Yet, here lay the jeep, undisturbed.

Jumping into the front seat, he put the key in the ignition. The engine purred. Relieved, he leaned back against the driver's seat before putting the vehicle into first gear. A sharp edge scraped his back. Lance turned around. The seat upholstery had a fine, two-inch slit in its back. He ran his fingers along the fabric. Nothing. Pivoting himself around for a better look, he pressed against the fabric. A pointed, red-tipped stone protruded through the upholstery. He touched his back, then inspected his fingers. Blood.

His eyes ached. He pressed his hands against his throbbing temples. He began shivering. *The stone blade. Is it poison-tipped?* He fought to fill his lungs but slumped forward. Shapes in the desert shadow stirred.

Two men dressed in desert camouflage and carrying automatic rifles walked up to the jeep. One man lifted Lance's head from the steering wheel; another seized Lance's backpack, rummaged through it, and pulled out a sealed, bubble-lined envelope.

Lance reached for the package.

The big man at the front of the jeep shoved Lance back against the seat.

Lance felt the stone blade in the upholstery drive deep into his back. His veins, his blood grew icy. The desert spun furiously around him blurring beyond recognition. He could not feel his feet, his legs, his chest. His hands shook a moment, then grew still.

Benjamin Franklin Medical Center   *1:02 P.M.*

Tetlow followed Kevin into his office. The room contained a great oak desk, computer workstation, leather couch, and rectangular Formica-top conference table buried beneath layers of printouts, disks, and CDs. Kevin pointed to the right corner of the conference table. "Pages twenty-six, twenty-eight, twenty-nine of the Principal Investigator's Quarterly Report and AEs, Protocol 1103-112. Draft four and five modifications are underneath." Pointing at the couch, "Earlier versions of HACV.V$_7$ outer layer synthesis, now outmoded." Pointing to the desk, "And I know every inch of that mess. Comes with having a photographic memory."

Tetlow studied his face. His eyes weren't dilated, his face wasn't flushed. There were no signs of psychosis or delusions, as far as she could tell. He appeared to be his same, sane, rooted, rational, brilliant self. But she had staked her career, her future, perhaps everything on him. And if he was cracking, she needed to know *now*, while the situation was still salvageable.

"I *did* see her." He took a suit hanging in the closet and laid it on the desk. "Twice." He told her about the runner along the river.

"Chasing women on the street? You're lucky there wasn't a policeman around." She leaned against a corner of his desk. "As for the woman in the lobby, Grayson's right. Lots of people pass through here. She could be an employee, a visitor, even a reporter."

A rap on the door. Tetlow turned to the man in the doorway: Peter Nguyen, PhD. The postdoc was skinny and had a round face and slightly cocked dark eyebrows that looked as if they were permanently frowned. His plain plaid shirt and slacks hung loosely on his frame beneath his oversized white coat—a reflection of workaholism, and a still-youthfully exuberant metabolism that happily burned Snickers bars and pizza without adding an ounce to his weight. He clutched a stack of stereographic molecular diagrams. "Sorry to interrupt. Doctor, we must talk."

Tetlow slid off the desk. "Dr. Kincaid has a press conference at two."

Nguyen nodded. "Yes, ma'am, but this is import—"

"It'll wait."

Kevin tried to signal his young postdoc to shut his mouth, but Tetlow blocked Nguyen's view. Nguyen said, "Ms. Tetlow, I just need a moment with—"

"Later!"

Nguyen stepped around her to Kevin, who was rolling his eyes and shaking his head. "Doctor, please don't go without seeing me first." He left.

Kevin picked up his white shirt. "Joan, unless you intend to watch me dress—"

"See you later," she said, then quickly departed.

Tetlow found Grayson back at her office. He was sitting behind her desk and smoking a foul-smelling cigar. Layers of rich smoke hung in midair as he tapped cigar ashes into a Styrofoam cup. "Mr. Grayson, this is a hospital. The alarm—"

"Has already sounded. What happens if Kincaid spots another 'ghost' at the conference?"

"Nothing is more important to him than his work."

Grayson smirked. "Mr. Loring has pledged the reputation and financial resources of this hospital, this health network, and himself to the Association to pass HR 601. There's behind-the-scenes lobbying. A very public advertising campaign in excess of $300 million, just for ads this one week, excluding the two-minute ad during the Super Bowl. And let us not forget Mr. Loring's biotech and allied research companies eagerly anticipating the bill's passage. New industries await birth, Joan." Grayson plunged the lit cigar into the cup. It hissed. "You've made noises for some time about moving up BFHN's hierarchy. It is within your grasp." He tossed the cup into the trash receptacle. "I must know whether Kincaid could jeopardize Mr. Loring's investment."

"We should have a contingency plan to divert the media's attention—just in case."

"See to it. And let's minimize our risk over the next few days. What's Kincaid's schedule?"

"Mr. Loring's party on Wednesday, of course. And a major presentation at the NIH campus on Friday. Should we cancel?"

"No, we want that kind of controlled environment. I mean interviews. Small, uncontrolled environments."

"Nothing like that."

"Keep it that way. No interviews, public or private."

She checked her watch. "It's getting late. Shall we go?"

"Not so fast. Four weeks ago, I left specific instructions for you to have Kincaid's files in order. You've done nothing. Has he perfected it?"

"I believe he is only days away."

"Without Kincaid's breakthrough, Mr. Loring's fledgling industries cannot come to fruition," he said, lowering his voice.

"I know the doctor. He's almost finished."

"How can you be sure? His work habits are sloppy. His notes are jumbled. There's no central file, on disk or hard copy, with the synthesis protocol. And no one, including his staff, seems to know the whole picture."

"Mr. Grayson, Kevin Kincaid can memorize virtually anything, instantly. His associates bring him pieces of the puzzle, and using that great brain of his, he assembles it. He's like a mainframe."

"Except that there's no backup. Joan, what if our 'central computer' was hit by a car? Or decided to sell his product to the highest bidder? Or," leaning in, "had a nervous breakdown?"

"It's not easy dealing with true genius."

"That's not my problem. You either get Kincaid's project files in order or you get him to re-record everything—from scratch. I'll give you one week." Grayson folded his arms. "And remember, Mr. Loring has partners. Some who tend to weigh life in terms of cost."

Rockville, Maryland

Anna Steitz stopped in front of a tiny storefront squeezed between a pizza joint smelling of grease and oregano and a sparse but trophy-laden Kung Fu studio. A computer-printed paper sign filled the storefront's window:

THE ANTIGEN ACTION COMMITTEE
JOIN THE FIGHT TO STOP GENETIC ENGINEERING!

Anna had suggested that Trent change the organization's name: *Antigen*—which was a common medical term for a foreign substance that stimulated antibodies. Trent had countered with a sardonic smile that it was appropriate that his organization's name could be confused with infection.

The storefront's worn wood and glass door stuck, then swung wildly open. The front room's peeling beige walls were covered with provocative blowups: dissidents in Athens who dressed like tomatoes to protest research permits for genetically engineered vegetables; protesters in Hamburg who sported bunny suits to challenge imports of genetically engineered soy; marchers in Ottawa who donned biohazard suits to protest standards for accepting genetically engineered food; activists in Milwaukee who dumped snack chips from genetically engineered corn in front of the local FDA office. A sullen woman with frizzy bleached blond hair sat behind an old gray metal desk. She inspected Anna's diminutive frame, from the short black bangs to the size-two shoes, then gazed into Anna's dark brown eyes. The woman shook her head. "You just made it," she said and buzzed open the back door.

The corridor beyond, utterly dark and only slightly wider than her shoulders, stopped at the foot of a staircase. By memory, Anna took the seven steps up to another door on the landing and entered without knocking. The room beyond was a cybertech garage: a concrete floor with computers piled on boxes and light filtering from monitors dangling from shelves. Four men and a woman sat on folding chairs around a partially collapsed bridge table. A wiry man chewing on peppermints pointed to an empty chair.

"I did not yet miss the phone call, did I, Trent?" Anna asked, her Bavarian accent still strong.

The man flicked another mint into his mouth, then focused on the telephone and accompanying scrambling equipment on the table. She decided to wait in silence, like the others.

Trent McGovern was the AntiGen Action Committee. He carried a resolve as prominent as his cleft chin. In his late thirties, tall, with wavy but thinning russet hair, his turtleneck sweater outlined his sinewy build. The muscles in his shoulders, chest, and arms were trained, tight, trim. For a big man, his movements were surprisingly quick—a cross between ballerina and puma. Anna had seen him full-contact spar with the master at the karate studio next door, and down the instructor with a vicious hurricane kick. At rest, Trent had a confident warrior's composure. Anna remembered how he'd been so very charming. He'd recruited her from Germany's Green Party. She'd been arrested in Hamburg. Broke and alone, she had been bailed out by Trent; they'd dined on bratwurst at a lovely little cafe, and he'd convinced her to join him. How different he'd been, then. As for the others, Trent had recruited Cameron from the Australian Gene Ethics Network, Penang from the Third World Network, van Helding from the Dutch Coalition for a Different Europe, Johnson from NOCLONE, and, of course, Mason and Morgan. Trent himself had spent years with Greenpeace before becoming irreparably disillusioned. The team around the table belonged to him; he, alone, controlled funding. Penang believed that their leader was wealthy; Johnson, that the man had built a blackmail network. None dared investigate those conjectures.

The phone rang. Trent lifted the receiver and activated the scrambler. "Yes?" His brows furrowed, then slowly relaxed. "Will he be there?" He paused. "We'll be up tonight." He hung up and announced, "The team's ready, but Loring's not there. And isn't expected."

"Where is he?" Anna asked.

"His jet's on the ground, so he's probably still in Wyoming."

Anna had never met any of AntiGen's shadow cadre that tailed Loring. From what van Helding had told her, they weren't people she would have wanted to meet.

"Too bad." Sylvester Cameron gave a big smile that featured two wide gaps between saffron-colored teeth. "Could've picked 'em off."

"Loring's the most prominent of the bunch, not the most powerful," Trent said. "Kill him, and another takes his place."

"One less to worry 'bout."

Trent swiveled toward Cameron. "You'd bring the full force of the Collaborate down on us. We're a mosquito on the lion's back. Bite too hard, we get swatted."

"It has been two years, Trent," van Helding said softly, his eyelids naturally droopy. Seeing Trent's jaw tighten, "I do not say to question, but when?"

"Soon." Trent said. "They'll be vulnerable through Kincaid. Any questions for now?"

Anna needed to ask—for her friend. "Have you heard from Lance?"

"Not in three days. Last I heard, he was in Mexico."

"Why?"

"He wouldn't say. He's a loose cannon."

"Has she been told?" Anna asked.

"Not yet. You're closest to her. Come with us tonight and tell her yourself, unless you think telling her will jeopardize the mission."

"Nein, nein. She is totally committed. Such news will probably make her stronger. But she will be very—what is the word?—apprehensive?"

"She has good reason." Trent glanced around the table. "We all do."

Benjamin Franklin Medical Center

Kevin distractedly drummed his fingers on the table as the auditorium filled with reporters. A liver-spotted hand from behind immediately covered his fingers. Another covered his microphone.

"Please don't do that, Dr. Kincaid. The mike will pick it up," Grayson rasped. "I have every confidence in you. But if the questions become too difficult, look to me." He patted Kevin's back and, cane preceding him, slowly moved toward the podium.

Stragglers clutching gourmet cookies sneaked into the smattering of empty seats. Kevin surveyed the assembly, hoping to catch just a glimpse of the woman with Helen's face.

"Cheer up, Kevin," Tetlow whispered in his ear from behind. "This is probably your last press conference till the bill's passed."

To Kevin's left, at the other end of the stage, was a podium and whiteboard. As the last of the seats filled, he searched the faces in the audience. She was not there.

"Good afternoon. I am Frederick Grayson, president of the Benjamin Franklin Health Network. I'd like to thank you all for coming today," he delivered in a deep, broadcaster's voice over the microphone. "Dr. Kevin Kincaid will be available for questions in just a moment." He scanned the audience. "The Association to Cure Genetic Disabilities is a not-for-profit alliance representing more than fifty companies in the biotechnology, manufacturing, and health service sectors—an alliance that seeks to promote germline gene therapy, so that one day, our children may never suffer from genetic diseases that cripple their bodies or minds. An alliance that wants to rid children of the genetic time bombs they carry—diseases like cystic fibrosis, sickle cell, Tay-Sachs. The Association, and the alliance of companies it represents, wants to eliminate genetic disease from the face of the earth, in our children's lifetime." He paused. "The Association wholeheartedly supports the U.S. House of Representatives Bill 601, which lifts the ban on germline gene therapy imposed in the years following legislation against human cloning. HR 601 will enable research for new medicines that may eliminate genetic diseases forever. More than thirty different grassroots organizations representing different genetic diseases support our efforts. A list is available in the lobby. Now, some people have criticized the Association for conducting a media blitz to pressure the Senate into passing HR 601. To this, we plead guilty." Holding up a finger, "But if it eliminates genetic disease in one child, it will be worth it.

"The Association asks only for the opportunity to allow companies to conduct *research* in germline gene therapy—to have the right to submit these new medicines to the Food and Drug Administration, the same as any pharmaceutical company. It will be years before we have cures, but if we don't have the courage to start the journey, we'll never arrive! And so, I'd like now to introduce Dr. Kevin Kincaid, the Neiman-Stepfield Professor of Neurosurgery here at Benjamin Franklin, and Director of Genetic and Molecular Therapy. Dr. Kincaid?"

Kevin buttoned his jacket and walked to the podium, freeing the mike. "Thank you. Back in 1995, W. French Anderson, the father of gene therapy and an innovative giant, once wrote in *Scientific American* that we live in the fourth revolution of medicine. The first was public health measures like sanitation to prevent rapid, widespreading disease. The second, surgery with anesthesia to help doctors actually cure illness. The third, antibiotics to fight infections and vaccines to eliminate viruses. And the fourth, gene therapy, with its potential to deliver genes into a patient's individual cells, to cure diseases otherwise considered incurable." He paced in front of the whiteboard. "We've come a long way. The discovery of DNA in 1942. Watson and Crick's elucidation of its structure in 1953. Gene splicing in the early 1970s. Rapid sequencing of DNA in 1977. The first patient undergoing gene therapy in 1990. Construction of the first human artificial chromosome, the HAC, by Harrington et al at Case Western Reserve in 1997. Cataloging of the entire human genome ten years ahead of schedule, made possible by J. Craig Venter, the brilliant scientist who kicked NIH's Human Genome Project in the butt to get it moving. The pace is dizzying. The technology, confusing."

Kevin drew a double helix on the whiteboard. "This represents strands of deoxyribonucleic acid molecules, DNA." He drew a circle around the double helix. "This is the nucleus, the heart of a cell." Drawing an outer concentric circle, "And this represents one of the 100 trillion cells of our bodies, each containing a complete set of blueprints, written on twenty-three pairs of threadlike, double-helix structures which we call chromosomes. Each chromosome is just a huge DNA molecule containing some 60 million to 250 million chemical bases, all built by just four chemicals: adenine (A), thymine (T), guanine (G), cytosine (C). A-G-C-T, a four-letter alphabet encoding the 30,000 or more information packets on these chromosomes— the genes—that define human beings to the smallest detail. Genes give rise to proteins. DNA designs life; proteins express it. Everything from brain cells to skin cells are all ultimately built from proteins specified in the DNA blueprint, using an RNA intermediary. Although DNA is correctly translated into proteins 99.999 percent of the time, just one wrong chemical base in one gene of one chromosome can condemn a child to a wheelchair, or lead to cystic fibrosis or muscular dystrophy. The only true long-term solution is to fix those genes.

"When your transmission's broken, new upholstery doesn't help. Creating replacement genes that can supplement, replace, or usurp malfunctioning ones is just the first step. Inserting these replacement genes into the proper place on a human chromosome is quite another. The daunting challenge is finding a vehicle, a way to carry the replacement genes into the heart of the cell, the *nucleus*, and insert those genes where they belong. We call vehicles that carry genes into the cell nucleus *vectors*. Vectors are the key to any successful gene therapy. But there are problems.

"Researchers have tried piggybacking human replacement

genes onto inactivate, non-disease-causing viral vectors. Like retroviruses. Or lentiviruses, similar to inactivated AIDS virus. Or adenoviruses, like those causing common colds. Or adeno-associated viruses, that help other viruses. Or inactivated herpes viruses. Some vectors have been known to cause mutations. Some work only on growing, dividing cells. Some are very inefficient. All existing viral vectors can only carry a few very small genes, often too few to be useful. Some are toxic. In years past, there have been significant setbacks, even patient deaths. Some at other institutions right here in Philadelphia."

He paused, looking over the audience. "Then there's nonviral vectors that are based on synthetic chemicals. A few have reasonably good rates of carrying replacement genes into human cells, a process called *transfection*. Yet none consistently carry their gene payload into the cell nucleus. And if the gene payload isn't delivered into the cell nucleus, then the gene therapy is doomed." He walked across the stage. "But, using a new vector developed here at Benjamin Franklin, BFV.Syn108, we've been able to insert two sets of genes into patients with brain cancer—genes that make the cancer more susceptible to chemotherapy. Early results look promising."

Kevin looked out across the audience. Compared to his new vector, BFV.Syn108 was as archaic as dinosaurs. But he'd been premature once before with another promising vector. That mistake had never become public. He would not risk it again. "The human body has two basic types of cells: *somatic cells* and *germline cells*. Somatic cells are nonreproductive cells, like those in your muscles, skin, lungs, liver, heart. Germline cells are reproductive cells: sperm or eggs. Fix somatic cells by somatic gene therapy and you cure the patient. But that patient will still carry that same genetic abnormality in the genes of their germline cells. The result? That patient's child may *still* inherit that genetic disease. On the other hand, with germline gene therapy, you cure the child before it's born, *and that child's descendants*. Now, we have several options for germline gene therapy. One is to modify the genetic composition of a patient's sperm or egg cells so that the genetic defect is not passed on to the next generation. Another is to modify the genetic composition of a pre-embryo or fertilized egg, and then place that back in a mother's womb. Both methods can cure the child, before it's born, as well as that child's descendants. These methods are all well and good for planned pregnancies, such as in vitro fertilization.

"But for 99.99 percent of the world's pregnancies, that sort of therapy would be just plain too late to do any good. So, for the rest of us, there is a third, more innovative approach—germline gene therapy *for developing fetuses while still in the mother's womb*. New breakthroughs in vector research are coming—breakthroughs that may enable us to perform this miraculous new type of germline gene therapy in fetuses, theoretically up to the end of the second trimester. Expectant parents would have months to identify and treat their unborn child's genetic disease. Radical, yes, but perhaps the most *human* way, the most *humane* way to eliminate genetic diseases forever." He stopped, center stage. "I'm proud to represent the Association to Cure Genetic Disabilities. I urge you to support House Bill 601 to lift the ban on germline gene therapy. Let's give our children a chance!" Half expecting applause, "I'll happily field your questions now."

A man with a graying goatee asked, "It seems to me that using germline gene therapy puts future generations at risk. So why do it, when there's scientists making progress on other gene therapies that don't carry that risk and can actually *cure* diseases like hemophilia?"

Kevin said, "Hemophilia is the exception to the rule. We can correct the biochemical abnormalities in hemophilia by producing clotting factor VIII, which only requires a single, tiny gene replacement. But single-gene replacement is rarely enough. Sometimes, the problem is overproduction of gene product, meaning that you'd need to fix *trillions* of cells. That's just not practical—now, or in the foreseeable future. So, in special cases, somatic gene therapy may work, but certainly not most of the time."

A man in a silk suit asked, "Isn't modifying genes before birth against God's will?"

"It seems to me that if God gave us the tools to fix things that are broken, aren't we carrying out His divine will when we do? Germline gene therapy is an example of man using the magnificent machinery that God gave us to work with." Kevin turned away from the questioner to the rest of the audience. "And while we're on the subject, let me emphasize that such thinking is an extremist view not shared by most of the religious communities. As far back as 1986, the National Council of Churches adopted an extensive policy statement on 'Genetic Science for Human Benefit,' approving genetic descriptive research. Now, while not specifically mentioned, I believe that germline gene therapy falls within the spirit of that statement. It's only natural for people to be afraid that fast-paced developments in genetics could outstrip common sense and moral values. In fact, the National Institutes of Health have been spending more than thirty million dollars a year for decades to examine precisely these ethical, legal, and social implications of genetic research."

"That's one view," the man followed. "But suffering is part of life. If genetic therapies eliminate suffering, they remove a natural condition that builds human character."

Kevin walked toward the man. "Bubonic plague, smallpox, malaria, typhoid fever, tuberculosis, influenza, ebola, AIDS. Do they build character?"

"Many of my readers believe that if there exists a gene for something like—like Down syndrome, then perhaps it's God's will, and that He had a reason for placing it there."

At the side table, Tetlow rolled her eyes. "Oh no."

Kevin stopped at the edge of the stage. "Have you ever spent time with someone with profound Down syndrome?" He glared as the man shook his head. "Well, I have. And let me tell you, it sure is hard to see God's divine will there!"

Tetlow and Grayson exchanged nods.

A woman on the far side of the auditorium asked, "Don't human cloning and germline gene therapy go hand in hand?"

"Absolutely not," Kevin declared. "Cloning is genetically *duplicating* physically identical human beings. I find it morally abhorrent to clone an entire human being, not to mention some very significant technical difficulties and, of course, the congressional ban in the opening years of this century, making it legal to conduct whole-body cloning. Germline gene therapy, on the other hand, preserves every child's uniqueness, eliminates genetic disease, embraces individualism. Cloning destroys all of that."

A clean-shaven young man asked, "Won't passing this bill increase the abortion rate?"

"I see the opposite. Because parents may have the option to prevent genetic disease in their unborn children, they'll be far less likely to seek an abortion for that reason."

Another reporter: "What about introducing dangerous new dominant genes that take over genes that occur naturally in people?"

Kevin faced the entire audience and smiled. "You see it all the time in science fiction movies and books: 'dormant' genes becoming 'dominant' and taking over. Amazing how you always have advanced civilizations that travel a light-year a minute, but can't seem to figure out how to fix flaws in their DNA—which is something we'll be able to figure out in the next generation or two. Warp travel is going to take considerably longer, don't you think?"

"Dr. Kincaid, both the UN and EC have declared germline gene therapy unacceptable," a man with gray hair and a thick German accent said. "Why should the United States not follow such policy?"

"Which documents are you referring to? The UN's Educational, Scientific and Cultural Organization meeting in Paris, 1997, that denounced human germline gene therapy? The EU's recommended ban? The Council of Europe's Recommendation 1100 expressly forbidding it? EuropaBio's declared moratorium? The AAAS—"

"All!"

Kevin paused. "No disrespect, sir, but traditionally, America's always been a leader in scientific research. NIH has funded vector research of new vectors *on healthy volunteers* for years . . ."

Tetlow smiled and whispered to Grayson, "Going well, isn't it?"

A man in a black suit said in a squeaky voice, "The Defense Advanced Research Projects Agency, DARPA, funds one billion dollars a year on genetic research." Turning to the audience, "Now there's this big push to lift the ban on germline therapy so we can change our children's genes. It's a government conspiracy to keep us in our place. What do you say to that, Doctor?"

Kevin grinned. "I like *The X-Files,* too."

A woman with red hair stood. "Before you said that we're years away from suitable gene replacement therapies. Yet ACGD is pressuring Congress into passing HR 601 right now. Why?"

Camera flash bulbs lit the silent room. *It's time,* Kevin thought. He said, "It's a bit premature, but our team here at BFMC is very close to developing the ideal vector. It's a quantum leap in vector technology. Safe, inexpensive, easy to administer, specific for any desired cell. But the key is the payload it can carry." He paused. "Every other vector I've previously described only carries at most a few thousand DNA bases into the cell. Enough for a couple of genes. But our new vector will be able to carry a payload a thousand times larger. Up to four hundred *million* bases. Enough to carry a full-sized pair of human chromosomes! We call our new vector HACV.V_7. HACV stands for human artificial chromosome vector. V_7 is the batch designation. HACV.V_7 will be able to carry a pair of artificial chromosomes that could supplement or replace not just one damaged gene, but a slew of faulty ones. With vector HACV.V_7, we may, one day, completely eliminate many inheritable genetic diseases in our lifetime!"

Cameras clicked. The room buzzed. One reporter shouted, "When?"

"Soon." He hesitated. "Naturally I can't disclose everything about it at this point, but I can give you a heads-up on some of our early work with animals. Specifically, *pxr1* knockout mice."

"Knockout mice?" someone shouted.

"I'll explain all that. Just please hold off your questions till

I'm done." He stepped to the whiteboard, completely erased it, then drew a stylized mouse complete with oversized whiskers. In the mouse's belly, he drew a circle with a pair of squiggly lines. "As you've no doubt noticed, I'm no da Vinci. So let's pretend that this is a mouse, that the circle inside it represents the nucleus of a typical cell, and the squiggly lines represent a pair of chromosomes."

He wrote $pxr1^+$ beside each of the lines. "The $pxr1$ is a particular key gene in mice. All mice need at least one healthy $pxr1$ gene," pointing to the $pxr1^+$ label, "on one chromosome to survive. Without it, they develop severe neurological problems that may include profound mental retardation, massive nerve injury and early death. In our lab, we removed healthy cells from a mouse embryo and cultured them." He drew a test tube in the corner of the board and connected it with lines from the schematic cell. "Now at the same time, we generated faulty $pxr1^-$ genes, which are $pxr1$ genes that don't work properly, and injected them into other embryonic mouse cells." In a separate diagram, he drew a squiggly line with $pxr1^-$ beside it in another test tube. Then, in the center of the whiteboard, he drew a large mouse and connected it to the diagrammed test tube with the $pxr1^-$. "We then injected the cells with the faulty $pxr1^-$ genes into different, healthy, pregnant, foster mother mice." Kevin drew two smaller mice beneath the central mouse and labeled each as $pxr1^+/pxr1^-$. "Next, we identified all offspring mice that had one functioning $pxr1$ gene and one faulty $pxr1$ gene." He pointed to the $pxr1^+/pxr1^-$ label. "We can call these *knockout mice,* because one of their genes has been knocked out."

"After that, we crossbred our knockout mice." He connected the two with lines, and then drew three new mice beneath the pair he'd already drawn. "That yielded three different types of mice offspring. Some mice inherited two healthy functioning genes," he said, writing $pxr1^+/pxr1^+$ beside the mouse on the left. "They were healthy as could be." He wrote $pxr1^+/pxr1^-$ beside the middle mouse. "Others inherited one healthy gene and one faulty gene. These mice were physically okay, because they had at least one functioning gene. But they were disease carriers, because they had one damaged gene." He wrote *pxr1⁻/pxr1⁻* beside the mouse on the right. "And still others inherited two faulty genes. The mice with two faulty genes all died within three days."

He pointed to the two mice labeled *pxr1⁺/pxr1⁻* in the row above. "Now let's go back to the knockout mice. We crossbred another batch and took chromosomes containing healthy, functioning *pxr1⁺* genes that we'd previously cultured." He pointed to the test tube with the *pxr1⁺* label. He drew a big circle that he labeled $HACV.V_7$. Inside the circle, he drew a chromosome labeled *pxr1⁺*. "We stuck those chromosomes on our new special vector, $HACV.V_7$. In a controlled experiment, we injected one hundred pregnant mice with our vector V_7 carrying chromosomes with healthy *pxr1⁺* genes and another hundred pregnant mice with a worthless placebo."

He stood back and paused, allowing the audience a moment to digest the information. "Here's what happened. Every mouse born with two faulty *pxr1⁻* genes whose mother had been injected with the placebo died within three days, as expected. But *none* of the pregnant mice injected with our V_7 vector gave birth to any offspring with two faulty *pxr1⁻* genes. And that's because our vector V_7, containing the life-giving, healthy *pxr1⁺* gene on a complete chromosome, found its way, in the womb, to the mice who would have died without it. And to accomplish that, our new vector had to have some remarkable properties that I can't discuss here. But the experiment undeniably proved that our vector was able to insert a complete chromosome into the nucleus of an animal's cell."

Another: "When will it be available to the public?"

"Sorry, but I'm not at liberty to disclose anything further."

Grayson smiled at Tetlow, then turned back to Kevin.

A woman with a recorder protruding from her hand asked, "Doctor, once we start using germline therapy for genetic diseases, won't we wind up trying to make our children smarter, stronger, or *better*?"

"That's a rather pessimistic view—assuming that the benefits we gain from any developing technology also must bring harm—a kind of 'slippery slope' leading to pure evil. What you're saying is that when we try to cure sickle cell anemia, eventually, we'll only be making children with blue eyes or whatever our ever-changing concept of perfection might be. It presupposes that we'll never recognize the difference between good and evil. I don't agree at all! The slippery slope is more like a broken-down staircase. Take a misstep and we'll feel it in our rump. The gap between restoring health by germline gene therapy and inheritable genetic modification, often called genetic engineering or eugenics, is enormous. *We will know the difference.*"

"How do we guarantee that?" a man ten rows back asked.

"Abstinence, antibiotics, vaccines—we make those choices every day. Each shapes future generations. Banning germline therapy today because we can't guarantee the safety of children two hundred, five hundred, a thousand years from now is like saying that people can't have children because they can't guarantee how their great-great-grandchildren will turn out."

A woman from the back of the auditorium: "What happened to the vector you worked on?"

"Hmmm?"

The woman emerged from a track-light shadow. "For years you worked on another promising vector, HACV.K_4. Could V_7 have the same problem as K_4?"

Kevin suddenly felt light-headed. Trembling, he leaned against the podium for support.

"How does that woman know about K_4?" Grayson snapped. "Nobody's supposed to know!"

Tetlow stared at the woman by the exit. "I've seen photos of her."

"Who is she?"

"Kincaid's wife."

* * *

Kevin steadied himself and fixed his eyes on the woman's. "Helen!"

The fire alarm screamed shrilly. Hospital security guards burst through the back doors and began emptying the room.

The woman disappeared through the back of the room. Kevin leaped off the stage after her.

A man in the audience screamed, "It's a bomb!"

Alta, Wyoming

The limousine wound cautiously along Ski Hill Road. The rugged, snow-covered summits of Mt. Owen and Grand Teton Peak loomed overhead. Kristin Brocks stared out the back window of her limousine. This terrain unnerved her: so sparsely populated and much, too much open space. And so high up. Was that why Loring had chosen to meet in such godforsaken country? Possibly, but her touch of agoraphobia and acrophobia had never appeared on any psych eval. She'd made sure of that. "How much longer?"

"We're there now, ma'am," said a guard riding shotgun in the front seat.

Signs reading "Grand Targhee Ski & Summer Resort" flanked the road as the limousine wound up the base of a mountain and, a half-mile later, stopped beside a booth. The driver held up credentials, drove up a private lane, and parked in a prime reserved spot beside the main lodge. "Ma'am, we walk from here."

Brocks had blond hair cropped unflatteringly short, white skin bordering on albino, and deep, glacier blue eyes shining from a face that had no makeup to enhance the remnants of her ancestral Danish beauty. She zipped up her parka, buttoned down the hood, put on her thick gloves, and glanced at her men. They surrounded her as she exited, their eyes constantly searching as she headed toward the lodge. Cold air bit her face and burned her lungs as she trudged to the staging area behind the main lodge, lined by antique Western storefronts. The aroma of croissant and Belgian chocolate wafted through frigid air. The woman's wary entourage deposited her at a tree-lined path with a gate marked "Snowcat Powder Skiing Only, Closed Today."

"The arrangement stipulates that we can't accompany you beyond this point," Brocks's lead escort said.

"Where's Loring?" she asked, her breath forming iced air.

"Waiting there now."

"Deployment?"

"Twelve sharpshooters confirmed on his side. We have fifteen, but numerical superiority isn't a tactical advantage here. You'll be totally exposed." He hesitated. "If I might speak freely, ma'am, why are you agreeing to meet him here?"

"Mutual assured destruction." She scanned the terrain. "Neither side can take out the other's director without sacrificing its own."

"Ma'am, that's not what I meant."

She squelched a smile. "By meeting him here, in an environment that he finds comfortable, we may create a false sense of security. One we can exploit."

"Risking the queen for a bishop is a poor gamble."

She looked at frost forming on her subordinate's brows. "We're out of time."

He nodded. "The lift will stop midway for precisely ten minutes. To extend that time, raise your right hand. To end it, raise your left. Director, if the situation deteriorates while—"

"I know."

"A chopper will be waiting for you at the summit." The man then spoke into a palm-sized transmitter. After a crackled response, the gate slid open. "Best of luck, ma'am."

Without looking back, she trudged along a wide, snowy path between towering evergreens. For weeks, she'd analyzed what she'd offer Loring if they met face-to-face: trades, concessions, bribes. What could one offer people who had everything? There was always the threat of exposure, but that would also expose the underbelly of her own organization's activities.

He stood at the end of the path by the chairlift: tall, vigorous, wearing a commissar-style fur hat atop gleaming silver hair, long woolen coat to his ankles, his hands clasped inside leather gloves. She focused on his weathered face, his dark brown eyes. Crow's-feet deepened with his smile. "Edwin Dixon Loring," he said, his voice rich and resonant. "Friends call me Dixon. Perhaps, when we reach the summit, you will, too."

The hard-looking, fortyish face that protruded from the parka hood cautiously smiled. "Kristin Brocks. Director, S and I, DARPA. You, on the other hand, may *not* call me by my first name, no matter what we've decided by the time we reach the summit."

Loring tisk-tisked. "I do so hate posturing."

"And I the cold."

"Among other things," he said with a wink as he scanned the mountain. "Lovely up here. *Open*, unoccupied, untamed mountains. So different from the warm confines of buildings and towers. And the view from so high in the sky, almost touching the clouds."

Rubbing it in my face, she thought, painfully remembering how, at age seven, she was lost for two days in Yellowstone. "You're very well informed."

"You sound overstressed, Ms. Brocks. It's no wonder, what with the in*tra*departmental rivalry and in*ter*departmental pressure in your agency and the Defense Department. And without the love and support of a good man at home. I can only imagine how painful it's been for you since your divorce. Someday, I'd like to meet that fool ex-husband of yours, who treated you so badly."

His comment confirmed her long-standing suspicions. She fought the urge to glare at him, and instead looked toward the chairlift. "Let's get going."

The chairlift started. Red, two-seat benches suspended by overhead cables whipped around the pole.

"Ever been on one of these?" he asked. Answering his own question, "Of course you haven't. All you do is stand a few feet in front of a chair as it rounds the pole, crouch a bit, and let the chair scoop you up. We go together. Which side would you prefer?"

She chose left.

"True to a knight's form. Keep your enemy by your sword hand."

They stood abreast as a chair whipped around, touched the back of their knees, cradled them, and began ascending the mountain. In seconds, they were half the height of great trees lining the ski trail. As the mountainside fell away, Brocks grabbed the strut joining the chair to the cable track. Her legs dangled over the edge of the chair. She dared not move.

"Don't be afraid."

She wanted to scream. "I'm—not."

Loring scanned the slope. "You know, Kristin, it cost a pretty penny to rent this mountain for the day, at the height of the season. In all fairness, DARPA should defray some of the expense."

Trying to ignore the openness, the mind-numbing height, she released her grip on the bar. "This was your idea. You can afford it."

"Yes." He beamed. "Yes, I can."

Brocks studied his face, a latticework of creases, each crease like a mark of success, built layer by layer, culminating in a quiet arrogance.

"As a sign of good faith, I thought we might start with a simple question," Loring said, gazing at her fingers clutching the strut. "We had an experimental facility in Mexico—"

"Which violates your organization's post-termination clause of the agreement with us that forbids you from using shared technology in facilities outside of U.S. borders."

Loring grinned. "The lab was developing new strains of—perennial wheat."

"But of course. Where?"

"Tiburon Island. In the Gulf of California."

"I thought that was a wildlife preserve. It must've taken some doing to get the Mexican government to cooperate with your *research*."

"There was an incident this morning. A trespasser might have obtained some potentially compromising information."

"We're not the only ones upset with you," she said.

"If you plan to release that information, think again. The facility's been dismantled, and Mexican officials paid off. The cover story will likely appear on the evening news." He shrugged. "Tiburon was obsolete, anyway."

"It was a crime against humanity."

"Let he who is without sin cast the first stone."

The chairlift halted. Their forward momentum caused the chair to rock gently.

"You've changed the rules of the game," Brocks declared. "We don't like it."

"Bureaucracy makes rules. Rules are poor substitutes for common sense."

She repositioned herself to face him directly, the chair swinging with her motion. "We want your media campaign stopped. Immediately."

"The public should be educated."

She ground her teeth and wrapped her arm tight around one of the bars. The chair gently swayed. "For years, both sides have kept quiet—to our mutual benefit."

"Change now is in *our* best interest."

"Any change should be gradual, preferably over at least one full generation. Not with a media blitz and Super Bowl blowout!" she barked.

"We're working within the system. Using the First Amendment. Aren't you proud of us?" He grinned as she glared. "There are precedents, Kristin. In the early 1990s, when Clinton first came to power proposing the government-run Universal Health System, the Health Insurance Association of America sponsored a series of ads. A working-class couple sitting at the kitchen table, 'Harry and Louise,' bemoaning how government health care would tear into their savings, wreck their lives." He unzipped his coat and reached inside.

"Easy!" she warned as her right hand reached for her automatic.

With two fingers, he withdrew a silver, insulated flask and opened it. A slightly sweet aroma wafted through the cold air as he poured a golden-colored liquid into the lid. He raised the

tiny cup to his lips, and drank. "Darjeeling tea. Custom blend."
He poured another cup, and proffered it. "Please. It will warm
you."

"I don't want to be warmed." She watched him finish the tea.
"Loring, we have the resources to reimburse you."

"It's not the expense. It's our commitment to working for the
betterment of man."

The chairlift started moving.

"Think we can't get to you, Loring? All of you? Antitrust,
IRS, SEC, OSHA, NSA, tar—"

"Look over the horizon, Kristin. You can see Idaho. I own a
biotech company in Boise. It's small, but community-oriented."
Leaning back, folding his arms across his broad chest, "I have a
feasibility study on my desk showing that it's more cost-
effective to relocate that facility in Malaysia. Which I'd prefer
not to do, but if I'm pressured, well—first, I'd get a call from
the governor, and I'd explain my position. He, in turn, would
call the senior senator, who'd call the Secretary of Defense,
who'd call your boss, who'd call you."

"We deal with pressure."

He raised his eyebrows. "Our members outright own or control close to $300 billion. When we speak, both White House
and Wall Street respectfully listen."

"If provoked, we can deal with you more *directly*."

He whispered, "We pay our assassins better."

The summit approached. Less than thirty seconds to dis-
mount.

"Let me phrase this as politely as possible," she said. "We
strongly urge you to reconsider. You know that we cannot allow
this to continue without response."

Loring swiveled toward her. His eyes were like cannons.
"You are the ones who've changed. We have always been on
this path. That should have been clear to you from day one.
You're in this up to your necks. So ally yourselves with us and
benefit, step aside and watch the future pass you by, or get in
our way and be dismantled!"

Brocks waited until their feet touched powdered snow. "You
may be better funded, but we move in technological vistas you

cannot imagine. And if you think I'm bluffing, remember that it wasn't Al Gore who invented the Internet—*it was us!*"

Lombard Street, Philadelphia

Sirens. Fire engines. Police directing people away from the medical complex. Kevin followed the crowd outside the hospital. His audience had spilled onto Lombard Street, snarling traffic. The mass of slowly surging bodies insulated him from the cold. Taller than most of the crowd, Kevin frantically looked out over the sea of heads. *Where is she?*

He spotted her: fifteen feet ahead and to his right was the back of a woman wearing a leather coat. Her hair, silken mahogany. "Helen!"

She drifted farther right. Kevin reached out and began shoving people aside. He closed in. Twenty bodies between them. Ten. "Helen!"

His fingertips touched her soft, calfskin coat. His hand clasped her slender arm. Heat shot through him as her body pivoted toward him. "Helen!"

Her gray-green eyes twinkled, a smile amplifying their glimmer. "Dr. Kincaid, delighted to meet you. I'm flattered that you know my name!"

She had smooth, supple skin, eyes bright as a kitten's, and seductively sloping cheeks. Beneath her coat was a slim physique with hauntingly familiar curves. Kevin brought trembling fingers to her face. The eyes, the hair—perfect. But her cheekbones were too high, her jaw too angular, her breasts too large. And her voice, too soprano, that of a woman in her late-twenties. Beautiful, but not his Helen Brewster Kincaid. *Of course it isn't her. I must've been crazy to even think it was possible.* "I'm—I thought you were—Helen. Stupid mistake. Sorry, sorry."

"But I am. See?" showing him her ID. "Helen Morgan. *Idaho Falls Post Register.*"

Eyes glistening, "Sorry again. I, uh, have to go."

The crowd surged, knocking her off balance. She tottered backward, wildly swinging her arms. Another shove sent her hurtling to the pavement beneath the stampede. Kevin seized her arm just before she disappeared, yanked her back onto her feet, and pulled her close. Nearly a foot and a half taller, he effortlessly shielded her with his body. "Let's get away from this." Tucking her into his arm, he plowed through the crowd and ducked into a driveway between sets of red-brick townhouses. Free from pressing bodies, he released her, but she clung to him. "Better?"

"Yes, thank you. Lucky woman—the one you mistook me for." She looked up before slowly, slowly separating. "Was that you by the river this morning?"

"Yes." He turned back to the crowd.

She touched his shoulder. "Don't go. We can talk."

"I—don't think we can."

"Because you can't, or you won't?"

"What would we talk about, Ms. Morgan?"

"Human artificial chromosome vector K_4."

He looked back. "HACV.K_4 is a secret. How'd you learn of it?"

"I have my sources."

"We buried that work years ago." He started away.

"Sometimes, things you bury come back."

He stopped. "No, Ms. Morgan. What we bury never comes back."

She stepped in front of him. "Dr. Kincaid, my career's on the line. The only way I could get here was with a one-way ticket and a promise to my editor to bring back an exclusive."

"You can forget that. Nobody's getting an exclusive. I signed a nondisclosure agreement with the Association and the Benjamin Franklin Health Network."

"Why would you do that?" she asked.

"So I could be ACGD's spokesman. Do some good. It's a standard contract and I understand their position. And as spokesman it's wise to be careful what I say and who I say it to. After all, the media is always looking for the cloud behind the silver lining, isn't it?"

"So you traded your rights so you could be their spokesman."

He cocked his head. "What's that supposed to mean?"

"You let ACGD tell you who you can and cannot talk to," she said.

"Nobody tells me that, Ms. Morgan. Nobody!"

"Apparently your contract does, Doctor. You just said so."

"It doesn't say *that*. And I'm not concerned anyway. What could they do—sue me? They wouldn't dare."

"Then there's no reason why you can't talk to me, is there?" She smiled. "It doesn't have to be an interview as such—just two people talking. Over coffee?"

"Some other time. Discretion, valor, and all that." He started walking away again.

"As important as you are, as independent as you think you are, you're still just their little compliant poster boy, afraid to stand on his own," she called.

Kevin turned back. Slowly released a faint smile. "Are you daring me?"

"Dares are good for us. They push us beyond what's comfortable and secure."

"Sometimes, right over a cliff."

"Which makes the thrill. As a scientist, you know the consequences of complacency."

He grinned. "So now I'm complacent?"

She crossed her arms. "Can you prove you're not?"

He studied every facet of her face. It wasn't his Helen, but it was close—so close to the image of his wife branded in his thoughts, living in his dreams. Fate was offering her face, or at least a reasonable facsimile of it. Why? "I'll give you fifteen minutes."

"An hour."

He smiled. "Twenty-nine minutes—with one stipulation. You agree not to compromise, malign, cheapen, or sensationalize my work in any fashion."

She beamed. "Absolutely."

In an alcove with Tetlow beside him, Grayson emphatically waved at the towering security guard in the surging crowd. The man recognized him, channeled his way through the exodus, and shielded his pair of superiors.

"The audience wasn't that large," Grayson mumbled.

"The entire hospital's being evacuated, sir," the guard said. "Bomb threat. We think the call originated in the auditorium lobby."

"We'll deal with that later. Have you seen Dr. Kincaid?"

"No, sir."

"And that woman who knew about K_4?"

"Her either, sir."

"If they're together—find Dr. Kincaid, immediately!" The guard disappeared into the crowd. "The conference is ruined," Grayson told Tetlow.

"Not necessarily. A bomb scare at a hospital during a press conference with the Association's lead spokesman guarantees solid network coverage this evening. And the media hates being victimized, so we might get a double-positive slant, both pro-Association and anti-activist. We could pick up five to seven points in the polls just on sympathy. And raise the dander of one or two straddling senators."

"Perhaps, Joan. I want you to find that woman. Who she is, who sent her."

"I'll get on it." Her teeth chattered. "It's getting cold."

His jacket was open to the whipping wind. "Fewer bodies, less heat. A guiding truth to remember as you rise through the ranks."

"Yes, Mr. Grayson. I'm wondering, though, if could she be Kincaid's wife. It's my understanding that the woman's body was—"

"No, his wife is dead!" He removed his fogged glasses and wiped them hard. "But whoever is posing as her ghost threatens us all."

They sat in the back of the luncheonette behind crammed tables and a stenciled window looking onto Twenty-first Street. Hand wrapped around steaming coffee, Kevin stared at the woman as she poured artificial sweetener into her tea, then quartered her cranberry-walnut muffin—exactly as his wife had done. Could she have made herself up to resemble Helen to gain his confidence? Maybe, but the resemblance could never be more than superficial. She could never *be* Helen. But while drinking in her face, his mind modeled it, like clay: working, reworking, shaping, softening, trying to make the transformation complete. If only it were Helen. Barring that, he would have been satisfied if he knew where his wife's body lay.

"They said there was a bomb."

"A hoax, Ms. Morgan," Kevin said, his eyes narrowing. "Do you reporters believe *every* inflammatory lie you hear?"

"You sound pretty cocky, Doctor," she snapped back.

"Haven't heard the boom, have you?"

"Maybe that's yet to come."

"Look, I know you reporters sensationalize your stories to sell advertising—"

"An old and very worn generalization, Doctor. I'd've expected better from someone with your intellect."

He leaned forward and thrust an accusing finger at her. "You journalists have fanned the flames at both ends—religious fanatics on the right, Greenpeace and anti-gene activists on the left. What's the angle of the week: a secret society purifying the racial gene pool? A government plot to mix our genes with aliens? Do journalists take some kind of perverse pleasure out of feeding people's natural paranoia, so that when science pushes us forward, you gleefully lead the charge back into the eighth century? Or does it all just come down to the almighty advertising buck?"

"Why did you abandon human artificial chromosome vector K_4?"

Kevin slammed his hand down on the luncheonette table. Ignoring the startled stares of the other diners, "What do you mean, *abandon*? It wasn't a baby left on some doorstep in the snow. It was an experiment. It didn't work. I tried something else. We call that science."

"Sorry. Poor choice of words."

"K_4 was supposed to be a secret. How did you find out about it?"

"A reporter can't divulge her sources."

"You'll have to—if you want anything more out of me."

Batting her eyes at him, "There's no need to be hostile."

"I am *not* being hostile. But it's not as if I didn't have good reason. You embarrassed me in front of the media."

She scribbled a few notes hastily on a pad. "Then I take it that you want me to go with what I already have on vector K_4, without your input."

"What do you have?"

"I'll remember to send you a tear sheet." She clicked closed her pen. "I hope you'll forgive any inaccuracies, large or small, that might appear."

"Hey! You're reneging on our agreement!"

She closed her pad. "Hardly, Doctor. I'm doing my utmost best not to compromise, malign, cheapen, or sensationalize—did I get your words correct?—based on what you're willing to reveal. Now if I release any erroneous information about your old K_4 vector which might lead to any unfounded rumors that could potentially jeopardize work on your new vector—V_7, was it?—then that wouldn't be my fault, would it?"

"Hiding behind 'absence of malice'?" *Not only does she use logic the same infuriating way that Helen did, she uses the same tone when she does it!*

"Make you another deal," Helen said. "I can't tell you who my source is, but I can tell you who it isn't—in exchange for information about K_4."

"There are legal and ethical limitations on what I can disclose."

"I can live with those limitations. If they're legit—and reasonable."

Kevin folded his hands. "How do I know that you won't give me the short end of the stick? You could tell me that Abraham Lincoln wasn't the source."

"Somebody around here has to show a little trust. It may as well be me." She sighed. "My source wasn't anyone who works or worked in your lab, or for that matter, anyone who is or ever has been affiliated with the hospital or any of your projects."

K_4 *was a secret. Virtually no one outside of those directly involved knew about it. If she's telling the truth—*

"How long were you working on human artificial chromosome vector K_4?" she asked, reopening her pad, clicking on her pen.

So much like Helen. Even the way she holds her pen!

"Come on, Dr. Kincaid, you agreed."

"Oh. Umm, uh, five years. I worked on K_4 about five years."

"And you started when?"

"A year or so after I came back East. About nine years ago."

"Which means you abandoned K_4 about four years ago? Why?"

He hesitated. "K series vectors work by transfection. That's a non-viral-mediated method for transferring genes into cells. What made the K series vectors unique was that not only were they capable of transporting complete, intact pairs of human artificial chromosomes, instead of small pieces of DNA, into a cell, they could transfer entire human artificial chromosomes, HACs, directly into the cell *nucleus.*"

"What's the difference?"

"DNA in the cell cytoplasm, that is, outside of the cell's nucleus, doesn't last long. When the cell divides, inserted DNA that's outside of the cell nucleus generally is not reproduced. It's lost. But when chromosomes are inserted, intact, into the cell nucleus, they become part of the cell's genetic structure. When the cell divides, the new chromosomes are carried into the next generation. The cell's blueprint, and the blueprint for that cell's descendants, have been changed, forever. K_4 was the culmination of that vector series." He watched her face grow warm, enthralled, like Helen's.

"Why did K_4 fail?"

"Because, Ms. Morgan, the inserted chromosomes tended to denature, that is, break apart when transfected into the cell nucleus. That left random-sized chunks of chromosomes, containing genes, floating haphazardly in the cell. In some cases, those chromosome chunks contained whole expression genes— genes that ultimately code for proteins. Worse, some of the chromosome chunks contained expression genes and pieces of regulatory genes that control expression genes. The 'on-off' switch, if you will."

"What would that do?"

"All too often, the genes coding for proteins had their 'on switch' left permanently on. This led to overproduction of some proteins that overwhelmed the host."

"I don't understand."

"Suppose you transfected a cell with an artificial chromosome that contained an important gene, say 'insulin'. Now, suppose that this chromosome broke into chunks in the nucleus. Suppose one of those chunks contained the gene coding for insulin, but that it contained only part of the genes controlling insulin production. The result? Without proper regulation, insulin production could run wild. A hundred times the normal quantity of insulin is lethal."

"So patients who received K_4—"

"No patient ever received K_4," Kevin declared.

She stared at him. "I don't understand. You just said—"

"All of our studies were performed in vitro, Ms. Morgan." She looked confused. He added, "Cell cultures grown in test tubes, in Petri dishes, or in tiny wells on a plate. All K_4 studies were performed on collections of cells. Animal cells at that. It's part of what we call the preclinical trial process."

"You're sure?"

"Don't you think I know the difference between cells growing on a plate and a living, breathing human being?"

"There's no chance that it could have ever been used on human subjects?"

Putting both elbows on the table, he leaned forward. "Wondering whether I run a horror show? Maybe mixing human and alien DNA?"

"Of course not, but—"

"I discontinued the project. Destroyed all the samples *myself,* according to standard operating procedures and guidelines set down by NIH and CDC." He realized that her question was legitimate: she obviously wasn't a clinical researcher and she had no way of knowing the details of the K_4 studies. Why was he so angry with her? Because she wasn't his Helen?

She rubbed her right eye.

"Are you all right?"

"The dry air's bothering me." A tear from irritation formed. "So why all the secrecy?"

"Some principles in K_4 also apply to the new vectors. BFHN's Board of Directors was concerned that if we released our findings on K_4, we'd tip off competitors."

"Your breakthrough vector, V_7, the one you hinted at in the conference. It's finished, isn't it?"

He shrugged.

"Your announcement at the conference made that an open secret." She smiled seductively. "You could send a poor girl from Idaho home happy. Which is not necessarily a bad thing."

"I made a mistake with K_4. I thought I'd perfected it. I spoke too soon. It was a debacle. So this time, Ms. Morgan, I'm keeping my mouth shut and all of the information," tapping his forehead, "stowed securely up here. That's where V_7 stays, until I'm certain that it works."

Helen leaned close to him. "I think that's an excellent idea."

He hadn't expected that. "Why?"

Her handbag rang. She opened the flap, removed a wireless phone, and answered it. "How long?" she asked. She nodded and hung up. "Dr. Kincaid, I have to leave." She stood, threw her notepad into her handbag, and slung her coat over her shoulder. She started toward the exit.

"Wait a second! You didn't answer my question."

She looked back at him. "Because more than your career depends on it."

Kevin abruptly stood. "What do—"

"Don't tell anyone—and I mean *anyone*—what was said here."

Kevin shook his head. "What a mistake it was talking to you. You might look like my wife, sound like my wife, even have some of her mannerisms, but you sure as hell aren't her!"

Helen glanced at the door, but took a step toward him. "If

you had the guts to get your head out of the sand and look beyond your own little protected world, you might see that I'm
the best friend you're ever going to have." She dashed out of the
luncheonette.

Senior Administrator's Office
BFMC   5:15 P.M.

Joan Tetlow found Grayson smoking another cigar when she
entered her office.

"What did Kincaid have to say?" he asked.

Trying to ignore the smoke that wafted across the room and
into her face, "The woman he met was Helen Morgan. She's
certainly no ghost, but she does bear a striking resemblance to
his dead wife, which Kincaid insists is just a lucky accident."

"I don't believe in serendipity," Grayson said. "Neither
should you."

"He says that this Helen Morgan is a reporter for an Idaho
newspa—"

"Who knew of K_4's existence. Not exactly public knowledge."

"That's all that Kincaid says she knew—when she came, and
when she left."

Grayson took in a mouthful of smoke. "And HACV.V$_7$?"

Tetlow pulled out a pocket recorder, hit the *rewind* button,
and waited a moment before stopping it. She put the recorder to
her ear, listened briefly, and again stopped the tape. "This is
what he said when I pressed him on the issue." She hit the *play*
button. Kevin's voice said: "Who the hell are you to tell me
who I can and cannot talk to? You may sign my checks, but you
don't run my life. Just remember, there are institutions that
would kill to have me. Some within walking distance."

She clicked off the recorder. "I've known him ten years.
Kevin Kincaid has always seemed like a burn victim, encased
in scar tissue, utterly incapable of touching or being touched by
anything or anyone—except for his work. I've never seen him
behave this way."

"We can reasonably assume that the reporter is the source."

"I believe most of his story," Tetlow said.

Grayson blew out a smoke ring. "Even so, he is covering for her."

"Why?"

"That, Joan, is what *you* are to discover. Kincaid is the only one who fully knows how to synthesize the new vector. Which makes it imperative that you get his files in order. I've already warned you once, I won't do it again."

"Consider it done."

"And find out who leaked K_4." Grayson straightened his collar. "I'll be back day after tomorrow to check on your progress. At which time I'll expect answers."

Adam's Mark Hotel, Philadelphia

Room 601. HR 601. Helen Morgan wondered whether the coincidence was a good omen as she slid her security key into the lock and opened the door. She flipped on the light switch. Nothing happened. "Crap!"

Hands outstretched, she groped across the dark room. A minty aroma filled the air—chocolate mints on her pillow?—as her fumbling fingers found her bed and guided her to the nightstand lamp. She turned it on.

"In for the evening?" asked a deep voice behind her.

She dropped her handbag, and slowly turned. Trent McGovern sat beneath a floor lamp, his feet propped on a table, his hands folded like a choirboy's. To his right stood Sylvester Cameron, his gap-tooth smile chilling, his dancing snake-tattooed arms flexing. To Trent's left, Howard Straub, her silent partner at the conference, vigorously chewed gum. And Anna Steitz swayed, jittery, by the TV halfway across the room.

Helen rasped, "I hadn't expected you here."

"Neither had I," Trent said. "Until Straub called."

Helen glared at Straub. She'd asked him, begged him to keep his mouth shut. The assignment was hers, not his, and she needed to complete it her own way. "Weasel!"

"Asshole," Straub returned. "Just like your brother."

"Children, stop fighting!" Trent snapped. Facing Helen,

"We're all family—*my* family." He smiled, glancing at Cameron, at Anna, at Straub. "Each of you was facing long imprisonments." He turned back to Helen. "Or death."

"You've found me useful," Helen said.

"Journalistic and auto theft skills, an eclectic mixture. Not nearly worth the trouble I went through rescuing you, and giving you sanctuary and purpose." He looked away. "And for what, Helen? So you could treat me like this?"

Helen gazed into Trent's eyes. She thought she saw disappointment, but Trent's mood shifts were notoriously erratic. The empathetic Trent often preceded the vicious version of him—sometimes changing on a single word. "Trent, I can ex—"

"It was too late to stop you." Trent popped a mint in his mouth. "The question now is whether it's too late to pick up the pieces."

That explains McGovern's presence, Helen thought. *Cameron's been brought in for additional muscle. But Anna? Why is she here?* She said, "Trent, it's going as plan—"

"You were supposed to seduce him. The man hasn't screwed for ten years. He'd have told you anything. All it called for was a little feminine guile." Slamming his fist on the table, "And you fucking wave a red flag in his face! Who gave you permission to announce K_4 to the world?"

"It was necessary."

"Bloody moron, she is," Cameron spat.

Trent strode across the room, holding his head as if it would explode. Anna dodged out of his way while Straub melted into the background. "When you trumpeted K_4, you blew your cover. You forced Straub to improvise, phone in a bomb threat, and disrupt the conference to prevent *them* from capturing you. How would you have escaped if Straub hadn't made that call? Or warned you during your little coffee break?" He approached her. "You've tipped off the Collaborate. Now, unless you're very, very careful, they'll use you to get to us." He pulled back his jacket to expose an automatic in its holster. "If this mission wasn't so critical—What's one to do with such a mischievous family member?"

"Kincaid may be naive, but he's not living in a fantasy world," Helen said. "He'd never have confused me with his wife. The trick was to use her face as the in. But that's not enough. We have to appeal to his intellect, too."

He put his face close to hers. "You're a clever liar. What's your real reason?"

"I'm telling you. It's the right way to get to him."

"Looks like you need a little disciplining." Trent looked across the room to Cameron and nodded. Cameron wheeled around and viciously slapped Anna with his open palm. Her head glanced against the bed. She fell to the floor. Cameron lifted her up and dropped her on the mattress. Anna sobbed. Her right eye was red, angry.

"You bastard!" Helen rushed at Cameron, who effortlessly pivoted around, swung his forearm beneath her chin, and locked her in a choke hold.

Trent shrugged. "We can't risk damaging your face now, Helen. But your friend, Anna?"

"She's one of us!"

"It's hard watching someone else suffer for your mistakes, isn't it? So, for Anna's sake, I ask you again: why did you make a spectacle of yourself at the conference?"

She struggled against Cameron's grip. "Because I had to know."

"Know what?"

"Whether he knew what the Collaborate had done with K_4. Whether he's one of *them*."

AntiGen's leader shook his head.

"Kincaid doesn't know. Trent, he really does not know!"

"A bomb doesn't know who it blows up, either. It just does."

"He's a doctor trying to stop disease!"

"He's responsible, Helen. Why should you care?" He looked deep into her misty eyes. "Of course. I see." He turned to Cameron. "Get the team. Go with the alternate plan."

"No!"

"Cameron, we go tomorrow. Two teams. One takes Kincaid when he's isolated after nineteen hundred hours. The other seizes the lab after twenty hundred hours. If he hasn't talked by morning, we kill him, then destroy the lab and computer system."

Cameron threw her to the floor.

"You've left us no choice," Trent continued. "You're too involved."

"You need me!"

"Not anymore."

"You're missing our best opportunity." She grabbed his jacket. "I know where V_7 is!"

Trent pivoted back to her. "Where?"

"In his head." She nodded. "He said so."

"Great! We'll pick him up tomorrow and—"

"Suppose he won't talk. Suppose he dies under torture first? Then what?"

"At least *they* won't have it."

Helen folded her arms. "Can you be sure?"

"What do you have in mind?"

"Let me bring Kincaid into AntiGen."

"Out of the question."

"Not only would he deliver us the vector, but think of it— their own poster boy speaking out against them. He could kill 601. Expose the Collaborate. It's what we've worked for!" She took a deep breath. "But take him hostage, kill him, and you solidify the public against us. HR 601 becomes law. Maybe even gives the Collaborate time to redevelop V_7."

Trent hissed through his teeth. He glanced around the room. Straub stepped away from the wall and tilted his head. Anna stopped sobbing, sat up sluggishly, pressed a hand against her swollen eye, and nodded.

"Could work, mate," Cameron voiced.

Trent shook his head. "The Collaborate will be watching."

"Yes, but they'll be cautious," Helen said. "As long as I'm out there *by myself,* I pose no overt threat. The risk to AntiGen would be minimal."

"But not zero." Trent bit on a peppermint. "Two teams will tail—"

"No! They'd be spotted. The Collaborate would clamp down around the doctor, pick off our people, and go straight for our carotid artery."

"Can you really prove to our angel of mercy that he actually serves the devil?"

"Yes." She wet her lips. "Have you heard from Lance?"

Trent looked to Anna, who said, "I am sorry, Helen. We do not think we will."

Helen's eyes started to tear. Her contacts burned.

"We heard it on the news. An 'accident,' they say. A toxic chemical spill," Anna continued. "Tiburon is quarantined, their cover story."

"Was Lance there?"

"His last reported position was in the Sonoran Desert, across the strait from Tiburon," Trent answered.

Helen's legs quivered, weakened. "But you don't know. He could still be alive."

"Don't count on it. And Helen, you still haven't explained just how you're going to prove your case to Kincaid."

Slowly, she whispered, "That's my problem, now, isn't it?"

Grinning, "I like your answer. So be it. You have forty-eight hours to bring in Kincaid. Fail, and he'll suffer an unforeseen accident by Friday. And if the Collaborate's on your tail, so will you."

Trent headed to the door before signaling his entourage to follow. Anna dragged herself off the bed, a hand still pressed on her eye.

"Let her spend the night with me," Helen suggested. "I'll put her on a train in the morning."

Trent said, "Straub will check on you both later." Patting Anna's shoulder, "It wasn't personal. I hope you understand. Keeping a family together sometimes requires discipline."

The door closed behind them. Helen listened, waited, then opened the door, peeked out, and checked the corridors and elevator bank. They had left. "Is the room bugged?" she asked Anna.

"Nein."

Helen crossed to the minifridge, wrapped ice in a washcloth, and placed it on Anna's eye. "I'm sorry. Trent is an animal." She sat beside Anna. "How did we become so submissive?"

"We both know. He is effective."

"Anna, I need your help. Aside from Lance, you're the only one I trust."

"You are my friend."

Helen patted Anna's hand. "We have to go to the District. Tonight."

"Why?"

"The patent attorney. But if Trent finds out—he'll kill us."

Loring Jet

E. Dixon Loring sprawled across his couch and stared out his cabin window to the hiss of rushing air. Low cabin lights cast a glare on the window as he gazed at the dark Rockies below.

How far Karbonville was: the old town was 20,000 feet below, 2500 miles to the east, and forty years away—but it seemed farther than that. Such an ugly place: mountain streets, corner bars, black-brick churches, small-thinking people whose lives consisted of hourly wages, brood-rearing, drinking, and brawling. He'd seen and fought his future early, at first by selling magazine subscriptions to people struggling to pay their electric bills. Later by learning to kick a football higher, straighter, and farther than classmates who bullied him for his frail physique. Placekicking: that was the revelation. Fresh, well-rested, he'd trot onto the field in the final moments to kick while the others, bruised, bloodied, and beaten, would drag themselves back for just one more play. He'd kick the field goal, win the game, and soak in the adulation, while the others who'd fought on the front lines the entire game were forgotten. Let others do the work. Reserve the killing blow for yourself. That was showmanship. That was power. It had bought him a scholarship to Penn State. An early career in investment banking that led to founding Comline Venture Capital, which financed successful biotech, software, and research companies that he leveraged. All the while, enhancing his showman image, surrounding himself with the beautiful and buxom, creating an image that focused on him so as to leave the rest of the Collaborate free to work, unencumbered by publicity. He put another pillow beneath his head.

"Excuse me, Mr. Loring," said a strikingly attractive woman with pale blue eyes. "Mr. Grayson is on the line."

"I'll take it here," he said, only glancing at the form-fitting skirt curved over her tight rear, swooshing as she left.

A six-foot screen snapped on with the satellite image of Frederick Grayson, his hands cradling his cane as he sat in the back of a limousine. "How was your tête-à-tête, Dixon?"

"Merlin, they're pathetic," Loring said.

"It would be a catastrophic mistake to underestimate them."

"That's near impossible." Fixing his pillow, "I caught a replay of the press conference."

"There's more." Grayson summarized the past ten hours.

"Disturbing, in light of the Tiburon incident," Loring said.

"The Agency could be involved."

"I didn't get that impression from Brocks. She knew about it, yes, but I don't think she's responsible. Besides, the foray at Tiburon reeked of amateurs."

"So does setting up a woman to impersonate Kincaid's wife."

"Good point. You know, Brocks said that there could be another player in all of this."

"Do you believe her?"

Loring sat up. "This is a delicate time for us. The closer we come to Implementation, the more vulnerable we become. Add in a wild card, you have the formula for disaster. Merlin, we've got to find the connection. That woman's the key."

"I suggest we observe her, discreetly. She'll lead us to her cohort."

"What if she doesn't appear again?"

"She will. She must." Grayson waited as Loring poured a gin. "Dixon, whatever Brocks said, whatever impression she gave, I do not believe that, as the time draws near, she will stand by and do nothing, no matter how strong our position. You might want to convene a Quorum."

"What for?"

"To accelerate the timetable."

Laboratory for the Research of Genetic and Molecular Therapy at BFMC

Kevin swiped his key card through the slot and put his thumb on the screen. The security system recognized him. The metal door clicked open as the LCD on the wall flashed: *Personnel in Lab: 0.*

The door closed behind him, immersing him in a silent, temperature-controlled darkness. Gradually, sounds of high-pitched hums from incubators and freezers filled the room. He'd spent the last few hours walking alone on the streets, trying to crystallize his thoughts. He needed a familiar place to think. This place was home.

The Helen he'd met certainly was not his wife. What had she meant by saying more than his career depended on keeping V_7 in his head? And the way she'd left just seconds before Grayson and Tetlow showed up? As if she'd been warned. As if she feared them. Tetlow and Grayson were bureaucratic obstructions, but menacing? They'd been generous to him over the years: unlimited equipment, manpower, funding. But then again, that was for his *work*, not for him. And the way Tetlow had questioned him about Helen Morgan, as if he had no life and weren't entitled to one. Maybe he had it wrong: maybe it was Tetlow who feared that reporter, not the other way around.

He flipped a series of switches on the wall. Banks of fluorescent overheads snapped on, and surged in progressive waves to the lab's distant recesses. Kevin's Laboratory for the Research of Genetic and Molecular Therapy was a three-storied temple of biotechnology. This floor, the second, was dedicated to isolating and identifying genes, and characterizing unique proteins. The floor above, for synthesizing expression vectors like $HACV.V_7$. The floor below, an animal lab where research products of the other two floors underwent preclinical testing in mice, rats, and, rarely, gibbons or chimpanzees. He looked out across a maze of workbenches, computer stations, and delicate free-standing equipment: biological safety cabinets for handling powerful chemicals; robotic arms for culturing cells; plate dispensers and universal microplate readers for assaying;

fluorometers for measuring unique colors cast by specially tagged genes and proteins; and microscopes connected to computers and mounted cameras for analyzing and photographing specimens. There were automated DNA sequencers, little tan boxes that shot lasers at fluorescent-dyed DNA fragments in an applied electric field, making it possible to identify thousands of chemical bases in minutes. There were reagents for analyzing and manipulating DNA genes and proteins: plasmid kits for inserting isolated genes into cell cultures; probes for forming hybrids with experimental DNA; polymerase chain reaction (PCR) kits to duplicate DNA; fluorescent dyes for tagging different human chromosomes; and blot kits for identifying DNA fragments and proteins. And, of course, software programs to analyze it all and compare it with databases from around the world. The physical and intellectual fruits of this floor were sent upstairs, where vectors were designed. All under his control.

Kevin stared at a workstation that contained a program for predicting protein structure. Uncle Dermot had boasted that he'd designed the ultimate program for that task, but did such a program ever exist? It had been ten years, and Kevin had never seen anything remotely resembling his uncle's claim.

"I thought you might be here," said a voice behind him.

Kevin froze, caught his breath, and turned. Behind him stood Peter Nguyen, his gifted postdoc out of the University of Pennsylvania, across town on the other side of the river. "Working late? And in the dark?"

"Where else would I be?" Nguyen said. "I'm surprised you didn't come here after the press conference."

"I had other things demanding my attention. Any problems here?"

"I'm not sure. After the bomb scare in the auditorium, security checked this place thoroughly. Very thoroughly. As if they were looking for more than a bomb."

"Such as?"

"I don't know, Doctor. They didn't take anything. Didn't disrupt anything, either. But they were definitely looking for *something*."

"Is that why you're still here? To see if they were coming back?"

"Maybe, in part."

"Well, apparently they're not. So it's late and you can go home." *And I can have some quiet time to think.*

"You hired me to be thorough," Nguyen said.

"I hired you because you're brilliant and have real insights into transfection processes." *That, and you're the only one in the lab I completely trust, because you've never asked for anything.* "So now that you've been suitably complimented, you can go home happy."

"There's nothing for me there."

Kevin sighed. "Man, do I ever know that feeling." Seating himself at a workstation, "It's been a year. Is there any chance she's coming back?"

"Divorce papers haven't been filed. So I suppose there's a chance."

"I don't know what's worse—knowing that there's a chance or knowing that there isn't."

Nguyen shoved his hands in his pockets and looked away.

Kevin remembered that reaction from Nguyen, just before learning of the K_4 debacle. "You said that you were still here *in part* for security. What's the rest of it?"

"We have a big problem downstairs." He hesitated. "With the *pxr1* knockouts."

Kevin charged the elevator at the far end of the floor, Nguyen three steps behind him. He pounded the *down* button. "Come on."

The *pxr1* gene knockout mice were the first animals that had successfully undergone germline gene therapy with vector V_7. From there, Kevin had used the vector to carry larger genetic payloads, building success upon success. But the *pxr1* knockout mice had been the first; they'd survived longer following V_7 germline therapy than any other living creature.

The elevator doors opened onto the ground floor. Kevin burst down a glazed brick–lined corridor, turned the corner, and opened a door into a room lined with cages. The odor of urine, feces, impending death assaulted him. Hundreds of cages were stacked against walls and in islands in the middle of the room.

Many were empty. Most housed frail white mice, staggering blindly, limbs twitching, or convulsing violently.

"Many are dead," Nguyen said. "The rest will be soon. It started while you were in surgery this morning."

Kevin stuck a finger between the bars of a cage and touched a quivering, furry ball. The mouse curled tighter. "All of them?"

"Like clockwork."

"You should've isolat—"

"There's no pathogen, Doctor. It's not viral. It's not bacterial." Nguyen stepped dolefully between the cage stacks. "I've taken random tissue samples. The pattern's the same: massive cellular lysis—as if the cells in their bodies are literally exploding." He dug his hands into his coat pockets. "At this point, I think we should assume the worst."

Kevin picked up an empty cage, wrapped his fingers between the bars, and pulled until its metal sides warped. "Damn it! All this time wasted!" He flung it aside and picked up another empty cage and hurled it at the brick wall, but it bounced off and only fueled his rage. He picked up a third cage and heaved it at the large window partition. The window shattered, showering the room with glass shards.

Nguyen retreated to the far wall and watched the large man's rage slowly dissipate.

Spent, Kevin surveyed the ruins surrounding him. Slowly, his hands covered his face. It was the end of everything. "V_7 doesn't work!"

ACGD Commercial #2—
"Germline Gene Therapy: Fix the Problem, for Good"

The following commercial aired on all major broadcast and cable networks the evening of Monday, January 20, and late night/early morning Tuesday, January 21:

[VIDEO]: Opening shot of a typical, middle-class suburban street of single-family houses. Close-up on one driveway: a frustrated man working under the hood of a new car. Dr. Kevin Kincaid walks on camera.

DR. KEVIN KINCAID (TO MAN UNDER HOOD OF CAR): What's the problem, Sam?
SAM: Something's always going wrong with this lousy engine!
KINCAID: What is it this time?
SAM: The distributor.
KINCAID: Why don't you give the car a new paint job?
SAM (LOOKING UP FROM THE HOOD): Are you nuts? What good would that do? You have to fix the problem!
KINCAID (TURNS TO CAMERA): Ridiculous, isn't it? You can't possibly expect to fix a car's engine by painting the hood . . .

[VIDEO]: Switch to sick child laying in hospital bed. Kincaid standing bedside.

KINCAID: . . . any more than you can cure many genetic diseases by giving chemicals and radiation. To cure the disease, you've got to fix the body's engines. You've got to fix the problem in each and every cell.

[VIDEO]: Transition to Animated Sequence: CGI (computer-generated imaging) of cell and center of cell (nucleus). Zoom in on center of cell, with crumpled white strings (chromosomes) and one black, misshapen string (deformed chromosome).

KINCAID (VOICEOVER [VO]): In the center of every cell in our body is a nucleus. The nucleus contains strands of DNA, called chromosomes. Each chromosome contains hundreds or thousands of genes made of DNA. These genes are the blueprints for our bodies. But sometimes, something goes terribly wrong.

[VIDEO]: Animated Sequence: Focuses in on misshapen black string.

KINCAID (VO): Just a few mistaken DNA molecules on one gene of one chromosome can mean a lifetime of suffering.

[VIDEO]: Split screen. Animated Sequence on left. Montage of sick children on right.

KINCAID (VO): Sickle cell, Tay-Sachs, beta-thalassemia, the list goes on. No matter what medicines we give these children, we'll never fix their engines—their genes. And the worst part is, if these children survive, *their children* will either suffer from, or carry the disease, too. Unless . . .

[VIDEO]: Full-screen CGI Animation: A bubble-enclosed white string (new chromosome) enters the cell and penetrates the nucleus. The white chromosome replaces the misshapen black chromosome.

KINCAID (VO): Unless we get rid of disease-causing genes in every cell. Replace them with healthy, working genes. "Why don't we?" you ask. Because, by the time we are born, it's probably too late. There are just too many cells in our bodies to fix. To save these children, we have to fix their genes *before* they are born.

[VIDEO]: CGI Animation: Pull back to reveal many cells with deformed black chromosomes replaced by healthy white chromosomes. Then hundreds of cells. Then the outline of an arm. Then the outline of a recognizably human fetus.

*Transition to Live Action: A pregnant woman receiving
an injection in the hospital. She smiles as a doctor with-
draws a needle (not seen clearly on camera).*

KINCAID (VO): It's called *germline gene therapy.* It will fix her
baby's cells before it's born. And her grandchildren will be
saved from the disease, too.

[VIDEO]:   Live Action: Wide-angle shot of healthy babies in nursery.

KINCAID (VO): But there are those in Congress who want to
deny you and your children access to germline gene therapy.

*[VIDEO]:   Healthy babies replaced by stills of children visibly suf-
fering from genetic diseases.*

KINCAID (VO): Call your senators! Tell them you want to permit research for germline gene therapy!

[VIDEO]:   Stills of suffering children replaced by healthy babies.

KINCAID (VO): Demand that your senators *support* House Bill
601!

*[VIDEO]:   Transition to pregnant woman, from previous scene,
now smiling in her hospital bed. Freeze-frame of her
cuddling a healthy newborn.*

KINCAID (VO): Give our children a chance!

[VIDEO]:   End Tag: Add supered letters to lower third of screen.
SUPPORT HOUSE BILL 601!
GIVE OUR CHILDREN A CHANCE![SM]
Paid for by the Association to Cure Genetic Disabilities.
Hold image for five seconds. Fade to black.

4

Helen drove the silver Pontiac down Connecticut Avenue. Anna squirmed nervously beside her. Street lamps marched along the avenue, each briefly and dimly lighting the car as it headed deeper into the city. Helen knew it was risky to steal a car for an unsanctioned operation, but she'd been careful to wear gloves with the fingertips sanded down, to use her home-made Lemon Pop to unlock the car's door, and to use a standard combination slide hammer and screwdriver to start the engine. She had no time for further precautions: it was four hours to Washington with a stop at Anna's Rockville apartment to pick up equipment, two hours for the mission itself, and three for the return. She had to be back in Philadelphia before dawn.

"When all is settled with Herr Doctor Kincaid, I am finished," Anna said, touching her swollen cheek. "When Trent recruited me, I accepted because I thought he was visionary. When did he change? Or was he always this way?"

Helen couldn't answer for herself, let alone Anna. Trent had found her two years ago: rudderless, bitter, running. He'd arranged for plastic surgery, a new identity, a channel for her rage. But he'd never fully assimilated her brother. What telltale signs had Lance seen that she had missed?

"Helen, are you certain of what we do?"

"I know Kincaid. His habits, his needs, his pain. I know how he'll respond to change."

"In playing the part of the doctor's wife, could it be that you have become too close to him?"

Helen looked to Anna, then turned back to the road. Supplied with hundreds of videotapes, voice recordings, and detailed documents, she'd spent the last year perfecting the image of Helen Kincaid: hairstyle, dress, gait, preferences, peeves, mannerisms, expressions, diction, personal philosophy—all that made Helen Kincaid unique to Kevin. All to enhance the natural physical resemblance that plastic surgery had provided. All to complete her mission. Was Anna right? Had she allowed herself to be drawn too close to him? She'd recklessly announced K_4's existence to prove to herself, not the mission, that she was not falling for a prince of the Collaborate. And now, here in the District, she was risking everything, again. "I know who I am," she said. *I just don't know what I am.*

Anna frowned, then reached under her seat, withdrew a laptop computer, and booted it. "You know him best. Will the Program convince him?"

A block behind them, a navy blue Toyota cautiously followed.

Laboratory for the Research of Genetic and Molecular Therapy at BFMC (Kincaid's Lab)

Peter Nguyen had watched Dr. Kincaid sacrifice three mice—two dying and one apparently healthy—remove the vital organs, section and stain them, and study the slides under low- and high-power microscopes. Cardiac, bone, lung, liver, striated muscle, nerve, kidney cells—all looked like tiny jelly-filled balloons dropped from a roof onto a sidewalk. "Massive cellular lysis," Kevin said, lifting his head from the eyepiece. "You're running cultures, aren't you?"

"Sure. But I don't think there's a pathogen."

"On what basis?"

"I found ten mice from another batch that had been mislabeled and mistakenly put in the same room as the knockouts for two weeks. They'd received the same diet, been examined by the same handlers, yet none of them have come down with the disorder. So if there is a pathogen, it isn't airborne. Other transmission modes seem even less likely." Nguyen shifted on his stool. "It must be associated with the vector expression system."

"But that was administered while the animals were still embryos. They're fully developed adults. Why would they be dying *now*?"

Nguyen hopped off his stool. "Maybe I could answer that if I knew V_7's full structure."

"I'll figure it out in time," Kevin said. He put another slide under the microscope.

"And what are the rest of us supposed to do till then? No one likes being left out."

Kevin rubbed his eyes, then put another slide under the microscope. "Everyone in the lab gets credit." He studied the slide. "We work together in teams, each tackling separate components of the vector. The harpoon, the cochleate cylinder, transport proteins—"

"But they're assembled in only one place, Doctor. *Your* mind."

"That's my job."

"But it's not good science, and honestly, Doctor, it's very disheartening. None of us working here ever gets to see the big picture. It's like working an assembly line without ever seeing the final product. There's accountability, but no personal satisfaction. None of us has ever seen HACV.V_7's full design." He paused. "The morale in this lab has never been lower. The line at the copier is so long, you have to take a number to photostat your curriculum vitae."

Kevin looked up from the slide. "Look how much we've accomplished!"

"The feeling is more 'Look how much *Dr. Kincaid* has accomplished.'"

"There's no reason people should feel that way."

"Forget the assembly line image. Here's a better one. Imagine working on a submarine: you're isolated, cramped, living in close quarters with no luxuries, no privacy, and you don't see anything other than pipes running through your tiny bunk or instruments at your duty station. You never see where you're going. You never know for sure where you've been. Except you, Doctor. You're the only one who gets to look through the periscope."

"If that's true, then why hasn't anyone come forward and told me? Ever?"

"You really don't know?"

Nguyen hesitated. "You're unapproachable."

"My office door has always been open—to everyone. At any hour for any reason."

"No, that's not it. You're unapproachable because you're—too brilliant."

"Peter, I'm not some egotistical bast—"

"You're always three steps ahead of everyone. Before anyone finishes their first sentence, you've analyzed their argument, formulated yours, proposed and analyzed their counterarguments, and devised your own winning rebuttal. It's intimidating."

Kevin remembered in perfect detail an early November morning recess: the caustic smell of burning leaves, the wind chilling his chest as it sliced through his skimpy cloth jacket. He was in fourth grade and standing inside the school's gates, where cracked asphalt met the school yard's only patch of grass. He watched nine boys play touch football with a makeshift ball of plastic and black tape. They'd let a new kid play, even though he was gawky and wore a tweed coat that hampered his running. There might never be a better time. Kevin felt his feet slowly shuffling over the bumpy, hard grass toward the boys. This time, *this time*, it would be different. He neared their line of scrimmage. They stopped. Jimmy Farber, the tall boy with the crew cut, turned toward him. He grinned. "Dumb-ass book-boy!" he yelled. Two of the other boys joined in. Then the new boy with the tweed coat. Then all of them. Kevin glanced down to his left: tucked under his arm was *A Primer on Solid and Plane Geometry*, a blue bookmark protruding from page 273. The image faded. His mind began showering him with painful memories, forcing him to relive shunnings that stretched from elementary to high school and a procession of college roommates who'd ignore him after the first week. Always alone: the curse of the gifted child. "I had no idea."

"Once the other staffers find out that V_7's failed, they're going to leave in droves."

**K Street, NW
Washington, D.C.**

"Are you in?" Helen asked.

SIA Security Systems' home page popped on Anna's laptop screen just as the car turned onto K Street. "Not yet," Anna replied.

Helen looked out the passenger window as the car passed an alabaster and glass building on a city block dominated by high-powered attorneys and lobbyists. "There it is." She slowed the Pontiac, peered at a small red sticker on the building's thick glass doors marked "Protected by SIA Security Systems," turned the corner, and parked between two minivans.

Anna typed in the building's address, and on-screen, pulled down a trio of small windows: a closed-circuit-TV view of the building's front lobby, a detailed schematic of the first floor, and a lock on the front-door security pad. "We have direct access to the building's security system, courtesy of SIA's mainframe."

"Oh, you're good."

"Trent thought so, too. He provided all my equipment. Strange it is that he has not called on me more often to use it."

"No stranger than him knowing where the Program is, and doing nothing about it." Helen put on tight, black gloves, then reached into the backseat and grabbed a canvas bag.

"You understand that I cannot guarantee overriding all security measures."

"Anna, we already agreed. If necessary, you're to cut me loose."

A gust of wind whipped through Helen's leather jacket as she opened the door. Traffic was sparse. The street deserted. She turned the corner and ducked into the target building's al-

cove. Thick glass doors sealed by magnetic locks led to the
lobby. Satisfied that the lobby was empty, she stepped to a keypad on the wall. Eyes scanning the street, she knelt, unzipped
the bag, withdrew a portable headset, and pressed it to her ear.
Anna's voice came through. "Got it," she answered, then
punched in an eight-digit code. Magnetic locks released the
right glass door. She slipped inside then slinked across the
building's lobby while trying to muffle her footsteps echoing on
the tiled floor. Bolts slammed behind her, their echoes reverberating across the atrium ceiling. She whirled around to the front
door. A surveillance camera swiveled slowly in her direction—
and stopped.

"Don't worry. It is me," Anna's voice sounded in Helen's
headset. "I sealed the main entrance. The building is empty."

Down K Street, behind the wheel of a navy blue Toyota, a man
placed a call on a scrambled digital phone. "She's entered the
building." He listened as a distorted voice responded. After
that, he asked, "And if she's discovered?"

Helen exited the stairwell on the fourth floor. The corridor had
maroon carpeting, matching walls, and was flanked by recessed
doorways with decorative windowpanes. A surveillance camera
panned the hallway, then focused on her.

"Suite 407. Third on your left," Anna's voice sounded in her
headset.

The camera followed Helen to a suite with gold relief on an
oak door:

DIEHL, TEASDALE & WILCOX

PATENT ATTORNEYS

After disarming the office's alarm system with the PIN number Anna transmitted, Helen unzipped the canvas bag and

pulled out a hand-sized cordless cylinder with a needlelike projection, and an electric pinch gun. She plugged the projection into the top lock and turned on the power. The device vibrated in her hand as the projection, the rake, struck up and down within the lock, opening pin and disc tumbler cylinders. Ten seconds later, the lock clicked. She repeated the process on the second lock, then swung the door open. Light from the hallway faintly lit a receptionist's desk. She took out a pair of night-vision goggles.

"There are no defense systems inside the office," Anna said.

Helen put on her goggles and cautiously entered. The suite had three offices, two conference rooms, and a bathroom off the reception hub. All doors were open, except for the one marked "Robert Diehl, JD." "I'm inside. No problems."

"Only Diehl's station will have the Program."

Helen went to Diehl's door and turned the handle. It was unlocked. She started to swing open the door, but stopped. It felt wrong, dead wrong: the Program was one of the Collaborate's key components. Certainly, the patent attorney needed a confidential copy, and according to Trent, the man had used it for years. But protecting such a critical piece of software with just a mundane security system? "Anna, it's too easy. We missed something."

"But SIA Security Systems does not—"

"I'm telling you there's additional security. I can feel it."

"Very well. Do precisely as I say. First, open the door, very slowly. No more than seven centimeters a second. Then gently, gently peer in."

Helen carefully turned the handle and pushed the door in, imagining a ruler along the floor, ticking off inches. The hinges released a long, guttural creak. "I'm in. What am I looking for?"

"Photoelectric cells. Motion detectors. Temperature sensors. The first two we manage. But there is nothing in your bag to defeat a temperature-sensitive sensor. First, scan floor and molding. See any small rectangular attachments to any wall, perhaps a few inches above the floor?"

Helen surveyed the room: a desk, chairs, couch, coffee table, and computer station against the back wall. Nothing along the molding.

"Now check the walls. Any unusual wall hangings?"

"Uh, no."

"Check electrical sockets. Sometimes they can be disguised as plug-in room fresheners."

"Nope."

"Check the ceiling. There should only be an overhead light, a smoke detector, usually round, and a sprinkler head. Anything else, tell me."

"Looks innocuous." Helen scoured the ceiling. "Nope, everything looks—wait! I see a small block pasted against the ceiling, but it also has a—looks like a cylinder embedded in it."

"A motion detector. A full 360-degree access with look-down. Probably quite sensitive."

"You can beat motion detectors with radio frequency interference."

"Not high-performance ones. It would take an expert. But you are there. I am here."

Helen clenched the door. "I'm going through with it!"

Anna exhaled. "You will have to move at the same slow pace. Two to three inches at a time. No sudden moves. How far is it to computer?"

"Oh, forty feet."

After hesitating, "You cannot cross the room in less than six minutes. Then, at the same pace, you must attach the CD-burner, access and download files, and erase signs that files were copied. Then, you have the same six-minute crawl back to the door."

Helen stared at the computer on the wall as if it were on the far side of Death Valley. Slinging one arm through the bag, she lay on her stomach and began the long, tedious crawl. Her finger-nails bit into the Berber carpet, each stunted pile loop a guide-post. She moved forward, thirty loops at a time. First one hand, then the other—maddeningly slow. Part of her mind concentrated on the systematic, autonomic crawl across the floor; part wandered, reflecting on how she'd come to this place. All roads led to Trent. How did he know so much about the Program? Why had he shared that knowledge with the rest of the Committee, yet forbidden them from stealing it, especially with the Collaborate so close to victory? What was Trent saving it for?

She grasped the base of a leather chair. Palm over palm, she pulled herself up, slithered into the seat, and buried herself in its contour. "Anna, I'm at the computer." Panting, "I don't know if I can keep this up."

"Boot the system. I will do the rest remotely."

"I thought we needed to attach the CD-burner to copy the Program files."

"I will download all Program files and remotely perform proper file wipes from here."

"If it's so simple, why didn't we plan it this way? What's the catch?"

"My laptop cannot accommodate two separate connections. To access Diehl's freestanding system, I must terminate the connection to building security system. I cannot download and watch your back at the same time."

Helen quickly pressed the PC's *power* button. "Do it."

Anna had stormed past Diehl's pitiful security measures, and was watching the last copy of his files float from his system to hers. When it finished, she eliminated any trace that the files had been copied. "Helen, you can shut it down, but do not power off until the computer says it is safe to do so. Otherwise, when Diehl boots his system, he will get a corruption reading." After Helen acknowledged, Anna terminated the link to Diehl's computer, then reestablished the connection to SIA Security Systems. "Oh my God!"

The observer in the blue Toyota watched two men in long woolen coats pull up in front of the building, punch in the proper codes on the exterior keypad, and enter. He'd already called his superior. Instructions would be forthcoming, he'd been told, so stand by. Another thirty seconds, and it would be too late. There was no choice: he opened his laptop.

Helen flowed from the chair to the floor, then spread herself across the carpeting and prepared for the tedious crawl across the room.

"Oh my God!" Anna blared in her ear. "You must have set off the alarm. There are two men in the lobby. They will be there in seconds. Get out! Now!"

Helen jumped to her feet and ran out of the office, slamming the doors behind her. She ripped the night-vision goggles from her face and scanned up and down the corridor. Elevators? No, she'd be trapped. The stairs? No, they'll come that way. Duck into another office? And risk setting off another alarm? She looked back at the elevators. "Anna, are they still in the lobby?"

"Yes."

"Take control of the elevators. Lock one at the lobby and send the other to the fifth floor."

"But—"

"Do it!"

Seconds later, the left elevator display changed from "L" to "2."

"Are they still downstairs?" Helen asked.

"Yes. Watching the elevator."

"Good." She opened the stairwell door. "I'll wait on the stairs, by the third-floor landing. Tell me if they enter the stairwell. When the elevator reaches the fifth floor, hold it there a few seconds, then send it back to the lobby."

"Why?"

"They'll think I'm taking the elevator down from the fifth floor. They'll naturally wait in the lobby for me to deliver myself right into their hands. But when the elevator comes back empty, they'll both take it to the fifth floor. With luck, I'll be able to walk right out of the building."

"Trent is right. You are the most dangerous of us. Am sending the elevator down." A moment later, "As you predicted, they are waiting."

"Disable the fire alarm," Helen whispered, trying to keep her voice from echoing in the stairwell. "This way, I can just scoot out the stairwell onto the street."

Anna paused. "They are taking the elevator."

"Now's my chance. Is the fire alarm disabled?"

She listened to pounding on the keyboard. "Damn! I cannot disable fire alarm!"

"It's okay, Anna. Anyone waiting out front?"

A long hesitation. "I do not know. The cameras do not look that far onto the street."

Helen faced the dilemma. Continue down the stairwell and exit onto the street, and she'd set off the alarm, removing any doubt that someone had breached Diehl's office. Exit the front lobby, she risked capture. "I'm coming out the front." She slinked down the stairwell, exited, and headed across the lobby. She checked her footsteps, her back, then hurried to the keypad and punched in the sequence. The magnetic locks released. She pushed open the thick glass door.

Two men in black coats stepped off the elevator. Each checked opposite ends of the corridor. "Nothing here," said one. "You check the stairs. I'll take the office."

Helen peered at K Street from the building alcove, but saw no parked cars, except for a blue sedan at the far end of the block, across the street. She bundled her coat and dashed down the street. Around the corner. And into her car.

"I looped the video in the surveillance cameras and inserted new time stamps," Anna said as they sped off. "There will be no photographic evidence of break-in."

"Great. Thanks for everything."

"You will drop me off at my apartment, and I will copy the Program, yes?"

Helen glanced at her watch. "We just might make it."

The man stood, arms akimbo, surveying Diehl's office. Computer, files, furniture, all appeared undisturbed. He looked up at the motion detector. "If only you were a goddamn camera."

His partner entered the room. "Didn't see nothing. You?"

"Same. Think anyone was here?"

"Dunno. But don't touch anything. I'll order up a forensic team. And a system analyst. They'll find—"

A whooping, high-pitched siren rang through the air.

Water rained from the ceiling and began dousing the computer, the desk, the carpet. The man glanced up at the overhead sprinkler spraying water onto the room. "The fuck did you do?" he screamed at his partner.

"I didn't do nothing!"

"It's all ruined. They'll blame us, you know!"

The partner wiped water from his face. "My story is that thing," pointing to the motion detector, "went haywire. Like the alarm."

"Works for me."

Helen turned onto Connecticut Avenue and noticed Anna staring out the window and mumbling to herself. "Problem, Anna?"

"I do not understand why I could not disable the alarm system."

"You were under the gun. We both were."

"No. I was locked out."

Kincaid's Lab

Kevin started, "You wanted to know the details of V_7? I'll show you."

Nguyen closed the conference room door then sat at the end of the long rectangular table.

Kevin, black marker in hand, was at the whiteboard on the far wall. "We begin with basics. The mouse: murine cells." He drew two concentric circles: a thin outer ring and a thick, double-layered inner one. "The outer cell membrane and the inner bilipid layer nuclear membrane," he said, pointing to each. Within the innermost circle, he drew pairs of squiggly lines. Beside them he wrote the number "20." "The murine cell nucleus, with its normal contingent of nineteen nonsexual chromosome pairs and one sex chromosome pair. This mouse is condemned to death because it's missing the critical functioning *pxr1* gene. We rescued these mice not just by supplying a functioning *pxr1* gene, but by inserting it on an *entirely new pair of chromosomes*, artificially generated here, in this lab. And by getting those synthetic chromosome pairs into the murine cell nucleus, where they became part of the mouse cell's genetic blueprint."

Nguyen listened attentively. Though this information was far beneath him, the preamble heightened his anticipation.

"Here are the five enormous hurdles our vector had to overcome." He wrote on the board:

HURDLES FOR VECTOR:
1. Carry a big DNA payload
2. Penetrate cell barrier membranes
3. Deliver DNA payload without disrupting cell
4. Have a 100% transfection rate
5. Deliver *ONLY ONE* payload per cell

"First, V_7 had to be able to carry a very large payload. Now, existing vectors can only transport twenty thousand to fifty thousand DNA bases, which is only enough for a few genes. We wanted our vector to lug entire chromosomes, which contain *millions* of DNA bases."

Nguyen crossed his arms. "Through both membranes? Quite a feat."

"Of course. For any vector to be effective, it has to be able to get the pair of artificial chromosomes through both the outer cellular membrane, and the even more formidable inner nuclear membrane surrounding the cell's DNA. If it can't get the payload DNA, whether it's genes or chromosomes, to penetrate both membrane barriers, it's a failure. Naturally, it also has to deliver that payload without destroying the cell," Kevin said, underlining point number three.

"You expect one hundred percent transfection? That's ten times more efficient than any other vector developed. You're demanding that a vector insert chromosomes into *every* cell."

"But if it fails to do so you can wind up killing the organism—or patient."

"You need at least one vector with a DNA payload for each and every cell you target."

"Exactly, Peter. But the last point is the most overlooked and most difficult hurdle to overcome. The vector has to be 'smart enough' to deliver only one chromosome-pair payload to each cell—and one pair only. If, for example, four or five individual vectors each delivered a pair of chromosome payload to the same cell, that cell would wind up with too many copies of a chromosome."

"Setting the stage for a cascade of genetic defects like—"

"Like Down syndrome, where patients have too many copies of Chromosome 21."

Nguyen considered the implications of the specs. "Somehow, the vector has to distinguish between cells that have been infused with the payload DNA and those that haven't. Otherwise, some cells will wind up with too many copies of chromosomes, and others won't receive any. V_7 overcomes all of these hurdles?"

Kevin planted both palms on the table. "This, Peter, is the work of art to which every person in this lab contributed. I was just lucky enough to assemble the pieces." He turned to the whiteboard and began drawing furiously with three colored markers. "This is what you've all built," he announced as he finished, "HACV.V_7."

Nguyen stared at the drawing and shook his head.

"Not what you expected, huh?"

"It looks like a burrito with a pointed tail and an oversized pea in its belly."

"V_7's design is an amalgam of concepts borrowed from nature, an MIT-AT&T collaboration, material researchers at Scripps Institute and UC-Santa Barbara, and NASA."

"NASA?"

"Think of V_7 as being like the old Saturn rockets, a three-stage delivery system, except that its payload is a pair of new chromosomes instead of astronauts." Turning to the whiteboard, "The first stage, a viral-like 'harpoon,'" pointing to the green tail, "developed by Pratt's team. And the attached cochlear cylinder," pointing at the red burrito, "developed by Gensini's team."

Nguyen studied the board.

"The harpoon resembles the tightly coiled proteins in HIV and influenza viruses. It has a barbed end that attaches into the cell's outer membrane, like a whaling harpoon. This, in turn, is attached to a cyclic peptide nanotube. The nanotube, in turn, is attached to a cochlear cylinder, which is a sheet of lipid rolled up like a crepe. The harpoon pierces the outer cell membrane with a small, temporary opening provided by the nanotube. The cochlear cylinder unwinds, exposing a small capsule," he said, pointing to the blue pea. "The capsule plunges through the cell membrane opening created by the harpoon and nanotube. And voilá, the capsule, containing the chromosome payload, is in the cell cytoplasm, and is ready for stage two."

"What prevents different vectors from harpooning the same cell?" Nguyen asked.

"The harpoon stays behind," Kevin said. "The nanotube collapses. The cell membrane seals around it. And," pointing to the red cylinder, "the rolled-up cochlear cylinder has sites on its exterior that are repulsed by the harpoon. In short, the cylinder won't unfurl and release the capsule if the cell has already been implanted by another individual vector."

Nguyen's eyes widened.

"The second stage is the capsule." Kevin drew a dotted line

from the blue pea and extended it into the cell, just outside the inner circle of the nucleus. "The capsule, or shell, containing the artificial chromosomes, is composed of copies of a single protein, bound together to form an icosahedron—a crystal with twenty triangular faces, like those in adenoviruses and polio virus. Except that this shell was designed to be broken apart by the cell's enzymes. A brilliant piece of biochemical wizardry, courtesy of DeVries's team." He wrote on top of the capsule in black marker.

"And that releases the capsule's contents, the synthetic chromosome pair, intact?"

"Right. Now, for the third stage." Kevin drew a convoluted pair of chromosomes in blue, and speckled them with black, green, and red dots. "Inside the capsule are V_7's payload chromosomes, neatly compacted, with the assistance of nucleosome proteins designed by Kanami's team," pointing to the black dots. "Once the capsular proteins are degraded, the DNA strands tend to uncoil into their natural state in solution. This stresses the nucleosome proteins holding the DNA taut, and ultimately, dislodges the nucleosomes." In blue, he drew a pair of classic, recognizable double-helix chromosomes.

"What are those?" Nguyen asked, pointing at the green and red dots on the previous picture.

Adding green and red squiggly lines to the chromosome pair he'd drawn in the outer portion of the cell, "The keys to it all. As we know, getting man-made materials through the cell's inner, double-layered nuclear membrane is tough—real tough. But the nucleus is constantly transporting its own molecules in and out of that membrane through its own complex pore system. Well, we've found a way to temporarily hijack the nuclear membrane's own pore system to get our artificial chromosomes inside the nucleus. We did it by attaching two essential proteins to the artificial chromosomes." Pointing to the green dot, "This one. A nuclear localization signal, NLS—a short sequence of amino acids that acts like a key to open the nuclear pore 'door.' And," pointing to a red dot, "the importin-gamma protein that drags the DNA right up to the nuclear pore. The artificial chromosomes are drawn into the nucleus like a kid slurping spaghetti. The last two proteins are courtesy of Chin's group and Horowitz's team." Kevin cupped his hands. "And there you have it. That new chromosome pair is now permanently part of the mouse cell's blueprint. When that cell divides, it'll make a new line of cells with twenty-one, not twenty chromosomes. Forever."

"Stunning!"

"You all made the music. I just conducted." Kevin stared at the drawing of the cellular nucleus. "So what the hell went wrong?"

Loring Estate
Santa Fe, New Mexico

Loring stared out his French windows. The 20,000-volume library in Santa Fe was the smallest on his estates, yet had the best view: a high desert plateau with uplifted jagged peaks to the horizon. He'd arrived before sunset and would be departing before sunrise. No time for anything but work as the last component of the Plan neared completion. Perhaps he'd see full Implementation in his lifetime. If not, well, he had the rare opportunity to both write and right history.

The grandfather clock chimed. The library doors automatically sealed. Two sets of dark drapes flew across and covered the glass vista. Soft, low-frequency music flooded the chamber to mask sensitive communications. Loring walked to a mirror on the far wall, tightened his Windsor knot, then placed his index and third finger beneath the right lower corner of the frame. A red light behind the mirror scanned his face from top to bottom, left to right. The lower half of the mirror grew opaque. A second later, white lettering flashed across the bottom:

FACIAL CAPILLARY PATTERN SCANNED.
EDWIN DIXON LORING RECOGNIZED.
INCOMING TRANSMISSION:
1 min 28 sec

He poured himself a sherry, then seated himself in a settee opposite the bolted doors. Red, blue, green lights scanned him. In the background, a faint A-minor chord chimed.

A rotund man with a silhouette reminiscent of Alfred Hitchcock's appeared sitting in the far corner of the room.

Loring respectfully nodded. "Mr. Bertram." He never knew where the transmission originated: London, Istanbul, Sydney, Kuala Lumpur, across town? The holographic intranet system kept transmission and receptive sites secret. Similarly, a projection of Loring's figure was appearing in one of Bertram's facilities, somewhere in the world. The difference: Loring's projection was real; Chairman Bertram's, a sham.

No one had seen Eric Bertram in more than twenty-five years. Loring had met him once almost thirty years ago, at a SciScan stockholders meeting. Bertram had been engaged in a hostile takeover, vilified by company management, investment bankers, and shareholders before he'd taken the podium. The man was obese, and had waddled to center stage amid catcalls and boos. But in a calm, melodic voice, he'd asked the audience seemingly innocuous questions, each answered by a simple, straightforward yes. Question after question, the answer always yes, yes. *Yes*. A half hour later, the podium had been transformed into a pulpit, the stockholders into a joyful chorus singing his praise. Three months later, he broke the company apart and extracted its assets.

Eric Bertram, a flamboyant and spectacularly successful investor and entrepreneur with more than $40 billion in assets, had been a lavish philanthropist until suddenly retiring from public view. Loring never understood why someone with so much power, so much wealth, wouldn't want to trumpet it to the world. The holographic image of the rotund figure was Bertram's appearance thirty years ago. Loring doubted that it bore any semblance to him now. Plastic surgery, weight reduction, hair transplants, the man could look like anyone.

"Your meeting with Brocks?" asked the holographic Bertram from speakers in the library ceiling.

"As projected, Mr. Chairman. They're terrified of implicating themselves." He sipped his sherry. "Their next move will be to step up surveillance. Probe for weakness."

"DARPA's forte is and always has been communications. Despite all our safeguards, they could penetrate our intranet. Which is why, for the next few weeks, we should minimize virtual conferences and rely on the couriers," Bertram said. "Your overall assessment?"

"The bill will be on the Senate floor next week. The ad campaign's in full swing. They've missed their window of opportunity."

"Buying large, expensive blocks of network airtime draws attention. DARPA should have known months ago. Why didn't they?"

"I don't know."

"We are *concerned* about the Tiburon Island incident."

"Mr. Chairman, I broached the matter with Brocks. I don't think they're responsible, but they may know who is. The investigation so far has shown nothing to disprove preliminary findings: a lone male intruder on the Seri reservation was detected and eliminated, but the helicopter carrying his body crashed in the sea. It was a shame we had to destroy the lab. We still don't know for certain whether security was sufficiently compromised to warrant that action. Nonetheless, it's done. At least we still have Delphi."

"I'll consult our contacts within DARPA."

"We could lose those operatives."

"Once 601 passes, we won't need them."

"Mr. Chairman, I suggest moving up the primary branch's timetable twenty-four hours."

Bertram's silhouette remained silent for a moment. "I don't think we need a Quorum to approve that adjustment. Proceed." Then added, "And the secondary branch?"

"I'll be checking on Kincaid tomorrow night. Personally."

Kincaid's Lab   4:47 A.M.

Nguyen lay sprawled across the conference table rhythmically snoring while Kevin stood with his eyes fixed on the whiteboard and his mind writing, erasing, reevaluating failed modifications. With V_7's intricate three-stage delivery system, the permutations for failure were enormous. But karyotyping had proven that the mouse cells contained the artificial chromosome pair transfected by V_7. Why then, after so many cell divisions, after such a long period in the mouse's life cycle, had there been such a catastrophic failure? Finding the cause could take years of testing. The flute began playing "Amazing Grace." His photographic memory again flooded his brain with agonizing images from which he could not escape. He looked at the clock: almost 5 A.M. Yes, a morning run would help. He tiptoed past the sleeping Nguyen. *Purge the body, purge the mind.*

Kevin's arms pumped. His feet pounded the West River Drive's frozen asphalt. Each stride carried him farther down the leafless tree-lined drive. A few yards to his right, the river flowed sluggishly. Freezing air that permeated his lungs brought pain, not euphoric release. Was it too much to expect his run to expunge the image of Helen and V_7's failure—if only for a moment?

The street lamps faded.

The sun appeared, bathing his path in light, in warmth. Trees grew thick, fragrant leaves. Clashing birdsongs arose from their branches. The air smelled warm, moist, lazy. And the river, now a tight, rippling stream, danced over a clear, pebble-laden bed filled with fat fish. Kevin stopped running. A towering man with short red hair, matching beard, and checkered shirt appeared beside him. "Can't catch fish with yer hands," he said, with a light brogue.

"Dad?"

Donnelly Kincaid, Sr., looked down at his sneakers. "I'm not wearin' hip boots, boy. Neither're you," he said. "No sport in catching fish with a net."

"I don't want a net, Dad. It's been so long. Can't we just sit? Talk?"

Donnelly slowly turned his head as if taking in a panoramic

view. "I know you're just dyin' to fish, but look around."

Kevin sighed. "You can't hear me, can you?"

"Beautiful, isn't it?"

He gazed up at his father. Proud, strong, defiant, brilliant—before life had pummeled him into submission. "This is Miller's Point. I'm eight. Donny's already—away. This is the last happy time the two of us will ever spend. Mom will die next month."

"Appreciate moments like this, son. Life goes fast," the elder Kincaid said. He produced a rod and reel. "Let's you and I get down to some serious fishing." He lifted the rod. "It's all in the wrist. First you slowly pull back, then you flick forward." Line and lure sailed into the creek. "Now reel it in." He demonstrated, bringing in an empty line. He placed a rod in Kevin's hand, "You try."

"I don't want to fish."

The man's great hands guided Kevin and his rod, but the line flew back. The lure snagged onto a branch behind them. Donnelly tugged gently at first, then began yanking. After a few tries, disgusted, he dropped the rod, traced the line to the branch, and tried to disentangle it. Instead, he pricked his fingers. "Sorry, son, it's hopeless."

Kevin stared at the leafy branch.

"We've got to cut it loose. I'll get the knife." The elder Kincaid took a pocketknife from his jeans and began cutting the line. "Sorry, son. Guess I'm not much of a fisherman."

Kevin's eyes never wavered from the tree. "That's it!"

The light faded. Leaves on the branch withered. Disappeared.

Puffs of warm, condensed breath floated across his view of barren branches. Kevin found himself lying prone on the icy asphalt. "That's it! That's it!"

Adam's Mark Hotel

Helen scrambled into her hotel room and checked the phone: no messages, fortunately. She dropped her coat and gloves on the floor, stretched out on her bed, and eyed the CD containing the copy of the Program she'd downloaded from Anna's laptop. Every AntiGen member knew that the Program had something to do with proteins. But now she and Anna suspected that it harbored significantly more information.

In seven hours the doctor would be in his usual Tuesday afternoon place—a place where he'd be vulnerable, open. That left her five to crack it.

She went to the desk, hooked up her laptop computer to the phone line, booted her system, and turned on the tiny camera atop her monitor. On-screen, icons popped onto a cirrus-cloud background. She clicked on the icon designed for file directories, slid the CD into a slot on the laptop's side, and began running the program. Setup "*.exe" files began downloading onto her hard drive. She minimized the file screen window as it worked, then went online and entered: www.uspto.gov.

Ten seconds later the link was established. The banner across the top of her screen read "U.S. Patent and Trademark Office" with options below it for searching the U.S. Patent Bibliographic Database. She chose "Patent Number Search." From the middle desk drawer, she pulled out a list of numbers: patent numbers processed by Diehl, Teasdale & Wilcox. She entered 9,408,571.

The screen answered:

Protein Kit for Analyzing Rat Membranes
Inventor: Walters, John
Assignee: Handot Biosystems

A slew of complex references followed, capped by an obtuse abstract.

She minimized the Internet browser window and restored the file managing window as the Program's setup elements finished downloading. The phone rang, a twirling trill of annoyance. She picked it up on the second ring. "This is your wake-up call," a whiny voice said to her.

"Straub, you weasel."

"That's no way to talk to your partner," Straub replied.

"Some partner. Ratted me out to Trent. Almost had me thrown off the mission."

"Trent told me to check in on you and Anna this morning."

"In the morning, not the crack of dawn. I'm going back to bed."

"Put Anna on."

She had dropped off Anna and the equipment at Anna's apartment—in Maryland. "She's asleep, nursing Trent's lesson. Let her alone."

"I don't trust you. You think you're smarter, better than the rest of us, just because you're a whiz at searching online. Big fucking deal. As far as I'm concerned, you're just some bitch Trent picked out of the gutter. Now, put her on. Or would you prefer I pay a house call?"

He doesn't know, she thought. *If he did, he'd have been here, gloating.* "Just a minute. I have to wake her." She had no time to conference-call with Anna on the same phone; Straub would know anyway. The only other phone in the room was her wireless. If she used that, Straub and Trent would trace it. Frantically she scanned the suite. The laptop! It might work—if Anna was online.

Helen cut the connection to the patent office, clicked on the outreach application icon, and hastily sent an instant message to Anna's mail address. *Come on, Anna. Be there!*

"The hell are you doin'?" Straub screamed.

A bleary-eyed Anna Steitz appeared on the laptop screen. Her movements were stiff, disjointed, a consequence of transmission inadequacies. "Hello, Helen. What did you—"

"*Wake up*, Anna," Helen said, picking up the phone, holding the receiver in front of the mini-camera. "Straub's on the line," she shouted, waving the receiver at the screen. She put the receiver next to the laptop's speaker.

Anna made an *oh* sign with her mouth. "Uh, tell him to let me sleep!" she yelled.

"Satisfied?" Helen asked Straub.

"Yeah, I guess so. Trent wants to remind you that you have thirty-six hours."

"I can tell time," she said. Then slammed down the receiver.

"Do you think he knows?" Anna asked.

"No, not yet. Get some sleep," she answered and ended the transmission.

On-screen, Helen opened the window and folder containing the Program files, and clicked the executable file. Her machine hummed briefly, then the screen flashed: Fully Installed.

She clicked "OK." A 15-item menu of unfathomable references appeared on the screen. Most of the choices, she suspected, were search engines for sophisticated biotechnology and/or genome databases. One, however, intrigued her. She clicked on the choice "U.S. Patent Office Interface." The screen replied: Program running.

Helen waited. Nothing happened. She shrugged, minimized the window with the Program supposedly running, reestablished her Net connection with the patent office, and entered the first number on the list: 9,408,571. "Stupid. I already searched that one."

But this time, the screen displayed radically different search results.

Kincaid's Lab

Kevin exploded into the conference room. "Up, Peter!"

Nguyen lifted his head and peered through sleep-encrusted eyes. "I'm not sleeping."

Kevin attacked the whiteboard. His surgical scrubs whooshed as he erased the last traces of $HACV.V_7$'s design, then began to draw a set of concentric circles representing a cell and its DNA-packed nucleus. "We've been sloppy fishermen." Not hearing Nguyen's "huh," he drew a barbed arrow into the cell membrane. "The problem is V_7's harpoon. We designed it to latch on to the target cell membrane and use nanotubules to create an opening sufficiently wide to inject the capsule enclosing the chromosome through the outer cell. We also designed the harpoon fragment to remain behind, stuck in the membrane, so that other V_7 complexes carrying chromosomes would recognize it, and therefore, not latch on to the same cell. Like a careless fisherman." Nguyen was staring blankly at him. "Don't you see, Nguyen? It's like carelessly casting your hook and line. Sooner or later it will snag. If you can't untangle it, you have to cut the line. But the *hook* just doesn't disappear. It's there, stuck where you left it waiting for someone or something to prick themselves."

"I just woke up. My mind's operating on a very simple level."

Kevin drew a line through the harpoon. "That represents the tip of the harpoon sticking through the cell membrane. It was designed to stay in place—apparently, too long, like a slow leak."

"But that wouldn't account for the massive cell destruction. The target cells have divided at least twenty times. Meaning that only a few percent of the cells in those mice were originally transfected by V_7. The vast majority of the affected cells are descendants of those original cells."

"Which means that *this* part of the harpoon," circling the portion of the harpoon outside of the cell membrane, "is responsible."

"How? An autoimmune reaction?"

"No, it's more mechanical than biological. I suspect that in a relatively uniform time frame the exterior portion of the harpoon dislodges, floats through interstitial tissues, encounters another cell, and punctures that cell's membrane. Then it moves on and punctures another cell—and so on. Like 'micro-daggers.' These 'micro-daggers' accumulate in the bloodstream and lymphatic system, causing widespread destruction over a prolonged period."

Nguyen's head tilted from side to side, as if weighing the theory. "Sounds bizarre. But if that's the case, what's the solution?"

"Redesign the harpoon. Make its protein structure less resilient, its amino acid sequence more easily degraded. The harpoon only has to be effective for a few days, not a lifetime. I already have some ideas for new harpoon structures developing in my head."

"Is this another Kevin Kincaid–only solution?"

"Oh, I want—no, I need your help. You and everyone else in this lab." He erased the board. Forcing a smile, "You're going to the NIH conference, aren't you?"

"Think I'd miss your speech?"

"Okay. We'll start a fresh slate on Monday. Full staff. I'll open up the problem to the floor. But in the meantime I want you to conduct serum assays and Western blot analyses in the mice for harpoon polypeptide sequences. Establish the validity of my theory and begin assays for possible antibodies to harpoon sequences, in case it is an autoimmune response. That should keep you busy for—"

"Ever," Nguyen finished. He nodded and left.

Kevin stared at the scribbling on the whiteboard. His mind had already begun synthesizing a modification of the harpoon that could potentially solve V_7's problem. But until then, how many more children would be waiting for a cure that might come too late?

Someone rapped on the door behind him. "Kevin?"

He turned around: Joan Tetlow stood in the doorway. "You're up early," he said.

"Busy week." she said, uneasily tightening her scarf. "I want to apologize about yesterday. I've been under a lot of stress. Grayson's pressuring me, and I supported him over someone who's put ten years of dedication and excellence into this institution. We've worked so well together for a long time. I don't want to jeopardize that."

"You went too far."

She took two steps toward him. "I, uh, I've been in touch with the Association's board. They're all very pleased with your news conference. We expect a strong boost in public opinion polls."

He stiffly clapped his hands. "I'm so happy for you."

"*Me?* You're responsible."

"It's *your* success. Yours—and Grayson's."

"You shouldn't feel that way." She touched his shoulder awkwardly. "We care about you, Kevin. All of us, especially me. Look at all I've done for you over the years."

"You did for me? For me? I'm not sure you *ever* did anything for me. For my work, yes, but not for me. And let's not forget that you and BFMC have done pretty damn well by me, haven't you?"

She sighed. "I already said I'm sorry."

Kevin folded his arms.

Tetlow softly said, "Kevin, I'm in trouble. I need your help."

"Your timing stinks."

"Loring and the board are demanding to see your progress. I know that V_7's files are in disarray, but—"

"There's just too much going on for me to handle that now. In a couple of weeks I can—"

"I need those files by the end of the week. Monday, the latest."

"Joan, you're asking the impossible."

Tetlow fixed her scarf again. "You remember that request you made last month for an additional five million in funding, over and above your budget projections? I believe you said you needed it for additional soft- and hardware, another full research team, new equipment?"

Kevin put his hands on his hips. "You said to talk to you in four months, around the start of the fiscal year. You weren't overly optimistic."

"We have a—special endowment. I can arrange for you to have whatever you want within ten working days—if I have those files."

"All of a sudden you can get the funding," snapping his fingers, "just like that? What's the hospital's general counsel supposed to do while you're sticking your hand in the cookie jar?"

"The funds involved are discretionary and justifiable, particularly in light of your recent publicity. I'm asking you—please."

He stared at her.

"My job is on the line!"

"Which justifies bribing me?"

"Kevin, please, you and I have had our problems, but," faintly smiling, "it took you almost ten years to break me in. Who knows how long it'll take for my replacement?"

He grimaced as he considered her offer. "All right. I can't do it myself with the conference this week at NIH, but I'll put Nguyen right on it."

"Nguyen? But I thought you were the only one who knew the formulation."

"I am," he said, rubbing his eyes, "but Nguyen and I were working on it this morning."

"You must have been up real early," she said. "Did the run help?"

He lifted his head and stared. "How did you know I went on a run this morning?"

"I saw you from my office. I've been there since four A.M."

Kevin remembered glancing back at the hospital shortly after beginning his morning run. Tetlow's corner office on the tenth floor had been dark when he left—and dark when he'd returned. *She's lying. How did she know? Did she have me followed?*

"So, I can count on receiving those files—"

"Peter'll have them on your desk by Monday afternoon."

"Great! What's your schedule for the rest of the day?"

"Rounds this morning. Then some time in the lab before seeing Donny."

"Yes, of course. It's Tuesday. I forgot." Tetlow stood and graciously smiled. "Thanks for being so understanding."

Kevin waited until Tetlow left the lab, then summoned Nguyen back to the conference room. "Peter, who have you told about V_7?"

"No one, Doctor."

"Good. Organize the files for Ms. Tetlow. She needs them by Monday."

"I can't do that and work on the harpoon problem simultaneously."

Kevin paused before answering. "Your work on the harpoon will have to wait for now."

"Are you sure?"

"Right now I've got to get our Ms. Tetlow off our backs. A couple of days on the harpoon won't make that much difference with the conference coming up. In the meantime, I can continue laying the theoretical groundwork for a fix. After all, that's my forte. You can start laboratory testing once I've worked out some possible approaches."

"Tuesday, then?"

"You bet." As Nguyen started to leave, he added, "And don't tell anyone about the design flaw."

"Uh-huh."

Kevin grabbed his arm. "I mean it. Not a word!"

"Okay, okay. Are you worried about PR fallout?"

Kevin released Nguyen's arm. "Yes, that's it. Bad press."

Dirksen Senate Office Building
Washington, D.C.

"Your eleven o'clock is here," the secretary's voice sounded over the intercom.

Senator Jordan DeRay checked his calendar and scowled. His appointment's mission was hopeless, but in deference to requests from some prominent contributors, he'd promised the man fifteen minutes. However, the senator from North Carolina had spent thirty-four years in Congress's Upper Chamber, served as a committee chairman, and, at his age, was obligated to no one but himself. Nothing on God's earth was going to make him change his mind. "Send him in."

An elderly man with round, black-rimmed glasses and a cane entered, his right hand extended, the other holding a notebook computer.

"Mr. Frederick Grayson, President of the Benjamin Franklin Healthcare Network, and representative for the Association to Cure Genetic Disabilities," the secretary announced.

DeRay stood, allowing the glare from the window overlooking Massachusetts Avenue behind him to blind his guest. He smiled, shook hands, and offered a seat. DeRay tilted his head and squinted. "Sir, have we met previously?"

"Not that I'm aware of," Grayson answered.

DeRay adjusted his steel-rimmed glasses. "Twenty-five, maybe thirty years ago. A fund-raiser in Charlotte?"

"I've never been to your beautiful state."

"No matter. Mr. Grayson, I appreciate your stopping by and hope we can come to a mutual understanding."

Grayson smiled politely. "Translation: I've as much chance

of procuring your support for HR 601 as God taking pity on a prayer from hell."

DeRay said, "I sponsored the ban on germline gene therapy in the first place."

"Times may change, sir, though people do not."

DeRay half smiled. "Especially this one, pointing at himself, when he doesn't have to—and knows he's right."

Grayson placed both hands on his cane. "Forgive me, sir, I misspoke. By people, I meant the human race as a whole. Essentially, human beings are the same today as they were two hundred thousand years ago."

"Mr. Grayson, I'd be happy to discuss anthropology with you some night at a fund-raiser, but right now, I'm a busy man."

"Perhaps there's some way the Association can help you find a way to reconsider your current position on 601."

DeRay grinned. "Sir, my coffers are filled, and I do believe my constituents will continue electing me after I'm dead."

"Perhaps one of our member companies can relocate in your fine state."

"The people of North Carolina would be grateful, sir. But not at the cost of their immortal souls."

"You make me out to be a devil, sir."

"Your next step would be to threaten to move one of your companies *out* of our fine state. You can, you know. But with Cary and Research Triangle Park, our bucket's already quite full."

"Senator DeRay, all we're asking is the opportunity to prevent genetic disease in children, as the March of Dimes does."

"No! You want to change the genes of unborn children while they're still in the womb! My God, haven't we done enough damage to the unborn in the last fifty years?"

"We just want the opportunity to fix Nature's mistakes."

"By introducing our own?"

"Senator, have you ever seen a child with cystic fibrosis?"

DeRay folded his arms. "HR 601 isn't about fixing genetic defects. It's about controlling people. Eugenics. And if tight-asses like the Germans and Swiss are scared of it, then by God, so should we."

Grayson glanced around office walls filled with photos of the balding senator with presidents in the Rose Garden, with chairmen of the Joint Chiefs of Staff, receiving awards and honors from universities and right-wing support groups from Cape Hatteras to Point Barrow. Grayson stood and extended his hand. "Thank you for your time, sir." After shaking DeRay's, he used his cane to slowly make his way to the door. Halfway there, he turned back. "Senator, after six illustrious terms in the Senate, wouldn't you like to leave behind a legacy?"

"I already have."

Glancing around the room, "More than scholarships, or awards, or buildings bearing your name. A real living legacy to the people of your state. Or, more properly, to the demographic groups who overwhelmingly vote for you. But demographics has a certain, oh, *color* to it, doesn't it, Senator? And certain *colored* demographic groups tend to feel that you don't represent them. And these particularly colored demographic groups tend to reproduce more rapidly than those groups a little less colored who do vote for you." He whispered, "Maybe not during your tenure, Senator. But inevitably your electoral base will become the minority."

DeRay gazed deeply into Grayson's eyes. They seemed familiar, as if housing a powerful truth. "And you possess something that reverses this trend?"

He hobbled over to a photograph of DeRay kissing a baby. "HR 601 is worded so as to permit germline gene therapy to restore normalcy. But no one has ever adequately defined *normal*, not to mention that it's politically incorrect to do so. That leaves the difference between *normal* and *enhancement* as a semantic interpretation suitable for exploitation."

"And just how does this benefit my preferred constituency?"

"Think ten years down the road, Senator. The middle class will be able to purchase certain advantages for their unborn children. Increased intelligence, strength. These will be expensive, probably beyond the financial means of *less desirable* groups. In time these advantages should more than compensate for the numerical superiority of those less desirable. In some districts one may correlate such differences along ethnic and/or racial lines."

DeRay whistled through his dentures. "Think I'm a fool?"

"This is no trap, sir. I am not wired. Have me searched if you wish. But remember, Senator, you can do more to shape the future in your favor with this one roll call than all of your previous votes combined over the last quarter century."

"There is a flaw in your demographics argument, Grayson. In theoretical terms, that is." DeRay swiveled his chair toward the window. "My base constituency, the folks who've sent me back here term after term, are good people, but poor, living off the land, never having the means to buy what you're hawking. They are *my* people."

"Precisely, Senator." Grayson sat down. "And that can be your true legacy."

DeRay patted his fingers before answering. "You make an interesting case but—"

"But not sufficiently compelling," Grayson finished. He again glanced at DeRay's numerous plaques and certificates adorning the office walls. "You've had quite a career in the Senate. I'm sure this room is but a small sampling of your many honors."

"That'd be a fair assessment."

"Thirty-four years on the Hill. Soon it'll be time to start campaigning again, assuming you plan to run for a seventh term."

"I'll never leave the Senate."

Grayson leaned on his cane. "More like you *can't* leave."

DeRay stared at his visitor, then chuckled. "I had no idea you were such a loyal fan."

"Senator, various investigative agencies are always dipping into people's pasts. These agencies, however, are easily intimidated by a six-term U.S. senator chairing one key committee and highly-ranked on several others. Now, we know that just in the past two years, you've squashed investigations into contract awards for the new interstate construction project around Charlotte and the collapse of two of the nation's largest banks, both headquartered in your state."

DeRay folded his arms. "I agreed to meet with you as a favor to some of the other party elders. I don't believe there's anything further to discuss."

"But they haven't yet looked into the Malaysian computer chip deal. What do you stand to gain for your part, two hundred thousand dollars?"

"I don't respond well to threats."

"Neither do we, Senator. But we haven't made any. Nor do we intend to. You don't build lasting relationships on fear." He sat back and slowly crossed his legs. "Sir, you're seventy-two years old, you've spent half of your life in the Senate. Despite all of your public protests, we know that, privately, you want to retire, travel, enjoy the rest of your life without the politics, the media, and the annoyances that go with them. You have considerable influence, but that decays with loss of power. Once you leave the Senate those investigative agencies will grow emboldened and begin looking into your past indiscretions. You become vulnerable. And if your enemies want you bad enough, they will get you."

The senator grimaced. "Sounds like retirement isn't an option."

"Quite the contrary, sir. The Association's influence extends to the highest levels. We will continue to protect you long after you've left office."

DeRay sat quietly a full two minutes before answering. "Not enough."

"Did you think that was all we were offering?" He motioned toward the desk. At the senator's nod, Grayson opened his notebook computer on the desktop, the cover facing his host. "Just a moment, please, to boot up and make the connection."

Three minutes later, when Grayson's knobby fingers had finished working the keyboard, he turned the notebook around. The senator studied the screen. It appeared to be an account summary statement.

"An account at the Zenstrasse Bank in Bern channeled through a dozen unbreakable dummy shells. Untraceable and safeguarded by our many security interests." Pointing at the bottom of the screen, "Notice the amount."

DeRay furrowed his brows at the figure: $102,843,711.40.

"The figure is correct, Senator. With that, you can establish a substantial charitable trust to see that *your* people have the financial wherewithal to purchase our—wares, and still have a very large retirement fund for yourself and your lovely wife. We consider it a worthwhile investment in America's immediate future. We would hope that you might convince others to see such possibilities, as well."

But why such an odd number?

"You don't recognize the figure, sir?" Grayson placed his cane across his chair. "It is ten times the amount that has found its way into your personal accounts over the last thirty-four years. To the penny, sir."

DeRay clenched his jaw, then slowly smirked. "Were such a thing to be true."

"I am a busy man as well, sir. Do we have an understanding?"

DeRay put his fingers to his lips. "I'll give your proposal the consideration it's due."

"Then the proposed legacy intrigues you?" Grayson asked.

"Yes."

"And it is desirable to make this your last term so that you can travel and enjoy your remaining years with peace of mind?"

"I suppose so."

"And is the figure you've seen adequate?"

DeRay nodded.

"Then the answer's obvious, isn't it?" Grayson shifted in his seat. "You'll undoubtedly want to verify this information through personal sources. Fine. However, the site will need to hear a confirmation from me by midnight, its local time, in order to fulfill this—order." Grayson checked his watch. "That gives you six hours to make your decision." He snapped closed the notebook and gathered it under his arm. Handing DeRay a card, "A secure number, where questions can be answered. I believe we've already shaken hands." He turned to leave.

DeRay waited until his visitor nearly reached the door. "Who exactly are you?"

Without looking back, "I believe I've introduced myself."

"No, you have not." He stepped around the desk as Grayson

opened the door. "I never forget a face, sir. Yours will come to me, sooner or later."

Chester County, Pennsylvania

Subdued sunlight filtered through barren trees as the Buick headed down the narrow two-lane road. Kevin knew every dangerous turn of this portion of Route 100; he'd driven it every Tuesday afternoon for ten years. The ride was quiet, comforting, and without traffic, he had a few uninterrupted moments for reflection, insights he might share with Donny. After many years, and after a fashion, he'd learned to interpret signs from Donny, signs that had to fight their way through miles of chemically unbalanced neural pathways.

The car approached a three-way intersection. To the left was an old narrow bridge across the Lenape creek. As he stopped at the sign, Kevin glanced at the passenger seat: it was empty. "Must've fallen under the seat." He threw the car into park, checked under the passenger seat, and pulled out a flat rectangular box wrapped in green and gold. A car let loose a jarring beep behind him. He checked the rearview mirror: a fat man in a black Mercedes was pounding on the wheel. Kevin warily turned his car left and drove slowly over the bridge while glancing behind him in the mirror. The Mercedes shot straight ahead, paralleling the creek, and disappeared around the bend.

The road led up a steep hill to a gentle plateau. After a quarter-mile he saw the familiar green sign swaying in the wind: Halloran House. He turned onto the long driveway. In spring and summer the grounds smelled like honeysuckle, with a garden boasting finely sculptured hedges, manicured croquet lawns, and long, lazy swings strung from tree branches. Now all was barren, dormant.

The main building, atop a small knoll, had white colonnades supporting the lower roof, which formed a long front porch, and sturdy, stucco walls surrounding its great wide old windows. It seemed more inn than institution. Kevin pulled into the deserted visitors' parking lot, took the gift-wrapped box, and walked briskly up one of the switchback ramps flanking the stairs.

"Hi, Karen," he called to the receptionist at the front desk. "Has he had lunch?"

"Uh-huh. He's in his room."

"I'll head right up."

"Oh, Doctor, *you* have a visitor." She pointed to a recessed, poorly lit waiting area behind him.

Kevin pivoted around: a woman stood, removed her overcoat, and walked out of the shadows. As the light touched her face, her gray-green eyes glimmered.

Genfutures Inc.
Gaithersburg, Maryland

Last night's break-in had drained Anna. As computer code swam across her screen, the flashing pixels taunting her bleary eyes, all she wanted was a quick nap, something her cubicle couldn't accommodate. Genfutures Inc. wasn't a bad place for a day job: flexible hours, good pay, work that honed her skills and kept her informed of developments in molecular genetics. All arranged, as a cover, by Trent.

The envelope icon appeared on the lower left corner of her screen, signaling a new e-mail. She clicked on the icon. It expanded to a window containing a message:

Anna, please see me on the fifth floor ASAP. Problems on the Korban project.
Steve Reynolds
VP Marketing
Genfutures Inc.

She deleted the message, yawned, then headed through the cubicle maze to the elevator. Eyes downcast, she waited. The doors whooshed open. She stepped in.

A powerful hand clamped down on her shoulder. Shaking, she slowly turned around. "Trent! What are—"

"Come with me."

The elevator opened onto the top floor. Trent, with index finger pressed into Anna's back, guided her to the stairwell and up the final flight to the roof. He slammed the door behind them. Cold air, channeled along the building's huge heating-ventilation-air conditioning unit, whipped across the rooftop and sliced through her dress. Ominous gray clouds hung low. He led her toward the Capitol in the distance—toward the roof's edge.

"What are you doing?" She straightened her legs, planting her feet in the soft gravel surface. Trent's thumb pressing at the base of her neck sent sharp, painful bolts down her spine.

Thirty feet to the edge. Twenty.

"Trent!"

Ten feet. Five.

"I think this is far enough," he said.

Her pain eased. She craned around. Her eyes teared from the cold as she watched him place his hands in his pockets. The wind flapped the tails of his coat. "Trent, I have to get back. Reynolds sent me an e-mail—"

"*I* sent it." He took two steps forward. "You're looking tired, Anna. Did you have a fitful night?"

"Yes."

"Spend the whole night with Helen, did you?" As she nodded, he approached. "What time did you get in?"

She retreated dangerously close to the precipice. "Almost nine."

"Anna, I care about you, just as I do for everyone in my Anti-Gen family. But if you keep lying to me—"

"I am not lying."

"Anna, I entered you into my world. I can exit you as easily." Taking a half-step, "Where was Helen last night?"

She glanced at the edge behind her. "In town. At Diehl Teasdale."

"You have the Program?"

"Helen could not convince Kincaid without it. And I trust her."

Trent bit down on a peppermint and inched closer. "The only reason your sloppy attempt worked was because *I* backed you up. Who do you think set off the fire alarm?"

She stepped back, lost her footing, and started slipping over the edge.

Trent snatched her as she screamed, dangling over the pavement sixty feet beneath her. "I should drop you on principle alone."

"Trent, help me!"

"The only reason you're not splattered now is because you pulled it off without alerting the Collaborate." He grabbed her forearm and strained. She slipped. He pulled harder. She reached out and clutched both of his arms. He yanked her up. Deposited her on the gravel roof. "Tell Helen she can show Kincaid the Program. Afterward, I expect it and any copies surrendered to me."

She expelled a sobbing, gasping *yes*.

He squatted beside her, reached out, and lifted her chin. "Wondering why I didn't want you to steal the Program?"

"Nnnnnein."

With the back of his hand he caressed her, cheek to chin. "Smart girl. I'll be in touch." As he turned away, he called back, "And remind her that she now has only thirty hours."

When he reached the stairwell, a gust of wind blew in her face, carrying with it Trent's mumbled words: "Because Kincaid will be dead shortly after."

Halloran House
Chester County, Pennsylvania

Helen studied Kevin's face as he moved ominously toward her. He stopped at the edge of her personal space and gazed down at her, taking full advantage of his height. This was her last chance for rapprochement. If he rejected her, he'd belong to Trent.

"What are you doing here? This place is way off the beaten track," he snapped.

"That's what the cabdriver said." She inched closer. "Sorry I had to leave like that. An emergency came up."

"Life or death, no doubt."

"But it did pique your interest, didn't it?"

"That remains to be seen. So why are you here, Ms. Morgan? The truth, please."

"To finish the interview."

"You're wasting your time. I've said all I'm going to say about K_4 or V_7."

"Actually, I was hoping to find out more about you personally: your motivations, drives, goals, reflections, past, those sorts of things."

Kevin smirked. "I'm not exactly the human-interest type."

"Oh, but you are the story. Down syndrome is your noble crusade. My readers would love to—"

"I don't give a damn about your readers. Donny's not a crusade. He's my brother and what's left of my family."

"I'd like to meet him."

"To put him on exhibit?"

"Haven't *you*, Doctor?"

"Now just what the hell does that mean?" he growled.

"Why, putting him in one of your public service spots for the Association, of course."

He stared at her. "How do you know that? Nobody knows that. The commercial hasn't been aired yet."

"Did you ever think that your brother might like to—" She stared beyond Kevin's right shoulder. A woman with smartly styled frosted hair and a fiftyish, luminous face headed across the main foyer. Her head sat atop a neck held obliquely six inches above a polished wood tray. Her right hand, palm forward, poked through a slot in the tray beside her ear while her left forearm was rotated ninety degrees behind her. Her spine was twisted backward so that her legs were positioned over her head, as if some enraged giant had seized her body and twisted it beyond undoing. Or she had been permanently fused in a bizarre yoga position. Helen had never seen someone so afflicted. She wanted to turn away but could not. Her eyes burned. She blinked rapidly.

From an optically directed control chip on a band around her head, the woman guided her motorized cart toward them. "Hey, doc!"

Kevin turned. "Wendy! How'ya doing?"

The woman looked to the box tucked beneath Kevin's arm. "There's chocolate-covered cherries in that assortment. Donny doesn't like chocolate-covered cherries. Be a shame to let 'em go to waste."

Smiling, "I'll leave instructions."

"Thanks." To Helen, "Hi. I'm Wendy Reymer."

Helen managed a raspy introduction.

Wendy motioned to Kevin with her eyes. He walked to her, bent down, and listened attentively as she whispered in his ear. He nodded, smiling at Helen.

"Got a Ping-Pong game coming up. Nice meeting you, Helen."

Throat thick, eyes watery, Helen watched the motorized cart chug to the back of the foyer. "What happened to her?"

"There's so many steps that can go wrong in the transition from embryo to infant. In Wendy's case, defects originated in her neural tube. Such a nice lady. She was condemned six months before she was born."

"But she's not, uh—"

"Mentally impaired? No."

Helen whispered, "Almost be better if she was."

"Why?"

"Because then she wouldn't have the capacity to understand what happened to her. I mean, how can you look at her and not be—when I looked at her, I didn't know whether to thank God that I've been spared or curse Him for screwing her over." She turned away.

"It's one thing to talk about genetic deformities in the abstract as 'vector target sites' or 'morality issues,'" Kevin said quietly. "Quite another when you glimpse the courage of the victims. Whatever story you're writing, Wendy belongs in it." He added, "So does Donny Kincaid."

She shut her eyes an instant in silent gratitude. Instead of the CD with the Program, she withdrew a pocket recorder from her handbag and turned back to Kevin.

Bypassing the ground-floor elevators, he led her up the main staircase. There were no institutional odors of urine, alcohol, and antiseptic; or vacant-eyed, partially robed patients wandering halls; or wild screams from locked, padded-wall rooms. The air smelled springlike. The walking or wheeled residents she passed along pastel-colored halls were well-dressed, alert. Sounds wafting through the halls were of laughter from private rooms, the upstairs game room, and off-key singing of "Sweet Baby James" in the auditorium.

"Let me give you a little clinical background of Down syndrome for your story. It's a genetic disorder characterized by the presence of an additional copy of the twenty-first chromosome. Instead of the normal two copies of chromosome number 21, people with Down syndrome have three. It's also called Trisomy 21. It's the most common cause of mental retardation and begins in the embryonic stage. It eventually results in reduced muscle tone and facial distortions, the most recognizable being an enlarged forehead."

She checked her recorder and nodded. "Don't people with Down syndrome generally live at home, become educated, employed, even—"

"Most, but there's a spectrum of severity. Many have IQs between fifty and seventy-five, mildly to moderately retarded. With training they function semi-normally. But Donny's retardation is profound—rare, even for Down's. He's in the bottom percentile. His IQ's below thirty. He can't feed or dress himself. He also has other neurologic complications, unrelated to Down's, from circumstances I don't want to get into." Continuing down the hall, "I brought him here—"

"After the fire that killed your family," she finished.

He stopped. "How did you know about the fire?"

"It's not exactly a state secret. Please continue."

He stared at her a moment, then resumed, "Here, Donny gets the best care available, but more important, he's part of a community. That's something he'd never get just being with me." They stopped at the last room on the right, a sign marked "Mr. Donnelly Kincaid Jr." Kevin looked down at her, then at her recorder. She turned it off and put it away. "Two rules," he continued. "One, while you're in the room, you can talk to Donny, or to me, but not *about* Donny as if he wasn't there. His speech is slurred, but sometimes he'll surprise you. Wait here," he said, ducking into the room. She heard an excited squeal. Then Kevin poked his head out the door and motioned her inside.

Donny's place was more hotel suite than hospital room: a fully furnished sitting room and furnished with a couch, dining table, and large flat-screen TV next to an adjoining bedroom with braces and assist bars in the walls.

"Donny, this is Helen Morgan. She's come here to talk to us. Say hello."

A squat man rocking vigorously in a chair chewed gleefully on a chocolate from the open box on the table beside him. The face that gazed at her was Kevin Kincaid's, though younger, stretched, flattened, with a Jupiter-sized receding forehead. The face bore a radiant smile reminiscent of Kevin from his old family movies—the movies she'd seen too many times.

"Hello, Donny," she said uneasily.

The man mumbled indistinguishably before opening his mouth for another chocolate. Kevin fed him a nougat.

"I'm sorry, Donny. I didn't hear. Could you say that again?" Helen asked.

Donny mumbled, his eyes wandering around the room. She smiled blankly as he spoke. Kevin sat down and massaged his brother's arm. Donny's head tilted as he uttered collections of vocal sounds. Kevin whispered in his ear, received a babbled return, then whispered more emphatically to his brother.

Helen slowly drifted closer to Kevin as she watched him interact with his brother: one of the brightest men on the planet showing no condescension toward one of the least intelligent. An instinctual warmth filled her, like the kind she felt at seeing a father carrying a daughter on his shoulder, or pushing his son on a swing. His back to her, Helen found herself reaching out to touch him, as if physical contact with him would somehow boost that warmth, would make that vision real.

Kevin glanced back at her as he was saying, ". . . Isn't that right, Ms. Morgan?"

Helen quickly pulled her hand back. "Uh, uh, yes. Sure." She glanced at her watch. He'd been talking to Donny more than half an hour.

Kevin patted his brother on the back and fed him a chocolate-covered caramel. "You can't understand him, Ms. Morgan, can you?"

"Sorry. Not a word."

He tilted his eyes up to her. "The speech pathologist assures me that the sounds he makes are just rudimentary attempts at spoken words. I've been told that, basically, when I listen to Donny, all I really hear is a projection of myself." He looked back to Donny. "I know better. If you listen carefully, you can understand him."

"You broke your own rule," she whispered. "You're talking *about* him."

He frowned. "That's what happens when I let down my guard."

She thought of the Program in her handbag, of her mission. But as she gazed at Kevin, at Donny, the Program grew less important. "I'll wait outside."

"Please, I want you to stay." Then added, "*We* want you to stay." He looked out the window. "My wife was very good to Donny. Like the mother he never really had. She was far better to him than I ever was. Ever will be." He drew in a shuddered breath. "Even I didn't think he was capable of remembering."

"Remembering what?"

"He's very happy to see you *again*. But he's also disappointed."

Helen Morgan returned his gaze. "I don't understand."

Kevin bit his lip. "He said that the last time you visited, you promised to bring the new baby."

Delphi

Marguerite Moraes looked around the empty gymnasium. Less than a year ago this playroom had been filled with toddlers running wildly in the creative dances, their laughter reverberating from the high steel-beam lattice overhead. Now it was silent, sterile, morose. She gazed through one of the great, iron-barred windows, beyond the helipad to the distant snow-covered hill. It was thirty miles from the school grounds to the nearest town, but it might as well have been three thousand. Though Marguerite was slim, athletic, once a marathon runner, she'd never made it anywhere near town before Delphi security officers had brought her back.

The surveillance camera in the far corner of the room swiveled toward her. The one in the near corner followed. It was unwise to stare out the window too long.

Loud grunting sounds echoed around the gymnasium. Marguerite turned to the little boy at the far end of the polished wood floor. "No, I haven't forgotten, Ethan."

He answered by grunting louder and emphatically pointing at the red rubber kickball tucked beneath Marguerite's arm.

Using a broad, toothy smile, Marguerite tried to mask her anguish. Ethan was so beautiful: almost four years old with gorgeous brown locks and adorable dimples. Three months ago the boy had an IQ beyond what the Stanford-Binet or WISC tests could measure. But the last seizure-induced stroke had ravaged his speech center. She prayed that it had also taken the last vestiges of his spectacular intellect so that he could no longer remember what he once was. Flicking her long, dark hair back over her shoulders, she knelt and slowly rolled the ball toward him. "C'mon Ethan. Kick as hard as you can."

Ethan looked intently at the red ball. His eyes suddenly lost their sharpness as if a black cloud had descended behind them. His head gently shook. His eyes rolled back. His arms, his legs grew tight, rigid. He fell to the floor. His entire body quivered.

"No! Not again!"

Chester County, Pennsylvania

"Thanks for driving me back to the hotel," Helen said as Kevin turned his Buick from the country road onto the main highway. "Have you and your brother always been that close?"

"Only after Helen—" He swallowed the rest of his words.

I have to pull him back onto familiar ground, before maneuvering him forward, she thought. She began with a question to which she knew the answer. "So Dr. Kincaid, are you hoping that germline gene therapy can correct Donny's condition?"

"No, you're confusing germline and somatic gene therapy," he said, eyes fixed on the road. "Germline cells are egg and sperm cells that unite to form a new organism. Somatic cells are nonreproductive cells, which is everything else: heart cells, nerve cells, whatever. In somatic gene therapy you change the genetic structure of nonreproductive cells—an area of lung or brain, such as for fighting cancers. In somatic gene therapy, no matter how many genetic changes you make to these organs, the children of these patients are still predisposed to inherit the same genetic disorder. But in germline gene therapy, you genetically alter the individual's egg or sperm cells, either directly or inadvertently through spillage."

"Spillage?"

"A vector that can't differentiate between germline and somatic cells. It alters both types."

"And in germline therapy?"

"The individual's offspring will carry the gene therapy's alterations so a patient won't pass on the genetic disorder to his children. Or by altering their unborn offspring, just after conception, in the embryonic stage. Or when the embryo is just a ball of undifferentiated cells, a blastosphere. Or while the fetus is still in the womb, perhaps as late as the end of the second trimester. Obviously, the earlier you intervene, the easier the process and the greater the likelihood of success. But any type of germline gene therapy can prevent genetic disorders from ever occurring."

She studied his profile: the muscles along his jaw and temple had firmed but the pain had evaporated from his eyes. "So somatic gene therapy would be the answer?"

"Yes. One strategy is gene augmentation therapy. In that case, the patient's cells are missing a gene encoding for a key enzyme or protein. So with a vector you supply the cell with the missing gene. A second strategy is targeted gene mutation correction. In that case the patient's cells have a mutated gene that's creating havoc. With a vector you insert the correct gene and remove the mutated one. A third strategy is targeted inhibition of gene expression. There you use a vector to carry a gene into a patient's cells that prevents mutated genes from being translated into faulty proteins. Of course, each strategy has enormous logistic and technical problems."

"Which would work for Donny?"

The car slowed as it approached a red light at the bottom of a hill. Stopped. "None."

"Why?"

"Donny has more than just an extra couple of genes. He has a whole extra *chromosome*. Short of inserting a vacuum cleaner into the cell nucleus to suck it up, I have absolutely no idea how to cure his disease at a genetic level. I'm not sure anyone ever will." He sighed. "There are drugs being developed that may one day counteract his biochemical imbalances, and studies have shown serious deficits in genes critical to proper development. But Donny is what he is. *I'll* never be able to change that. Maybe someone someday might find a way to build upon my work with expression vectors."

"*Expression* vectors?"

"Basically there's two categories of vectors. Cloning vectors, designed to insert a piece of DNA into a cell strictly to reproduce the new DNA over and over and over, like a virus. And expression vectors, used to insert the DNA into the host cell to make that cell function like normal."

"Like your V_7?"

"You know that I can't tell you anything about V_7."

"Have it your way. Frankly, it's irrelevant to my story."

He glanced at her. "Just what *is* your story?"

Helen repressed a smile: she'd made *him* ask. "There's a maelstrom swirling around you, Dr. Kincaid. Germline gene therapy is evolving into an across-the-board divisive issue. It's worse than the abortion issue because this one could destroy the foundation of civilization." Kevin chuckled. "It's true," she countered. "I've been out there ten months."

"And I've been out there ten years. You may have splinter

groups on the righteous right and radical left who oppose germline therapy for any reason. But people are starting to support it."

"With the abortion issue, religious and conservative groups oppose it while liberal-minded groups support it. But on the germline issue both extremes oppose it basically for the same reason. And that's only what you see aboveground. My story's about what's below." The car changed lanes. "Doctor, this theater has three other players. To start with, the government."

"You working with the reporter at the press conference? The *X-files* fan?"

"You laughed when he said that DARPA had spent a billion dollars on genetic research. Well, I have documents obtained through the Freedom of Information Act that show that the government's spent more, *a lot more* than that. DARPA in particular! And then there's eugenicists looking for racial purity. What they've lost through intermarriage they intend to restore by the kind of selective breeding germline gene therapy might one day make possible. From neo-Nazi Aryans to African-American purists, they're all well-funded and waiting for the technology to become available."

"Does your story get the front page all by its lonesome or do you have to share it with alien invaders and JFK clones?"

Helen turned, touched his arm, and whispered, "Something else is out there, Dr. Kincaid. Something a lot scarier than the government, the lunatic fringes, or even terrorists for that matter. What exactly it is, I don't yet know."

He shook his head. "You're chasing a shadow."

"There are times when I think you're right." She closed her eyes. "God, I've been on the road so long for this story! I don't even have a home anymore. I'm broke. And you know what the worst part is? The loneliness. Dinner at McDonald's for one. The not-being-touched. And the only man who's looked at me in God knows how long, only did so because I looked like somebody else." Feeling his eyes on her, she lay back in silence, allowing the *clump-clump* vibration of rubber on asphalt road to filter through her cushioned seat. Tears formed in her eyes as she realized that she'd said it more for herself than the mission.

"Ms. Morgan, do you have—plans for tonight?"

"I'm supersizing at Mickey D's."

After a long silence, he said, "I can get you in someplace nicer."

"Another table for one?"

He cleared his throat. "Let me rephrase. Would you like to go to one of the world's finest restaurants, tonight, with me?"

She opened her eyes. Turned to him. "Because I remind you of your wife?"

The car slowed, stopped at a red light. His mouth dry, he gazed into her eyes. "Because you remind *Donny* of my wife. He was more animated today than, well, that's worth the price of a decent meal."

"How about I trade that in for more info on V_7?"

"Don't push your luck."

Her mind played a collage of his faces: from continuously looped home videos with his family, from photos at schools and in professional societies, from his first gaze at her. *It's working.*

BFMC

"Table for two. This evening, first seating," the voice said.

"Thanks again for fitting me in so impossibly late," Kincaid's voice responded.

Tetlow clicked off the recorder on her desk. At last, the tap on Kincaid's office line had proved useful.

Le Bec-Fin
Philadelphia   7:59 P.M.

Crystal chandeliers, like diamond-studded broaches, reflected and refracted their light, bathing the restaurant in brilliance. A great mantled fireplace overlooked the elegant room of Louis XVI furniture and tables with Bernardaud china, Schott Zwiesel stemware, and exotic flowers. A delicate Mozart selection masked the sounds of tuxedoed waiters and busboys pampering patrons. Ornate mirrors provided the illusion of size for the intimate twenty tables. Helen sat beside Kevin. Her long, silken mahogany hair framed her small nose, high cheekbones, and gray-green eyes. A tight, black, shining satin dress with a low, square neckline accentuated her figure. Bringing a forkful of *galette de crabe* to her lips, she said, "This is scrumptious." Pointing at his full plate. "Your meal alone is a hundred and fifty dollars, and you haven't touched it."

"I'm not hungry."

"You'll excuse me if I am." She touched the corners of her mouth with her napkin. "You might be looking at me, but you're seeing her."

"I've read that people choose prospective mates based on subconscious appraisal of symmetry. What we interpret as beauty is really just facial and body symmetry, which our minds interpret as measures of health and vigor."

She demurely smiled. "Deciding how symmetrical I'll be in bed?"

"No two symmetries are the same. No matter how subtle, there's always imperfections."

"Care to list mine?"

"What I'm trying to say is, when I look at you, I see Helen Morgan, not Helen Kincaid."

"Because of my imperfections?"

"Because of your differences."

She interlocked her hands like a bridge and balanced her chin on them. *"Par exemple?"*

"The resonance in your voice. The way your jaw skews to the left when you chew. When you look at just the right angle, a hint of melancholy in your eyes."

"Maybe that's a reflection of your own."

A busboy appeared beside Helen and took her plate. As he removed Kevin's plate, he accidentally touched the china to Helen's water glass. The stemware tipped over, spilling onto the table. The busboy apologized profusely, dabbed a damp spot on the tablecloth, and hastily departed with Helen's glass. He returned a moment later with a fresh glass for her. With a tiny brush, he whisked crumbs from Helen's side of the table into a tray and exited just before a waiter presented a plate of *filet de boeuf* to Helen and *mignon de veau au citron* to Kevin.

"So, Ms. Morgan, what is your story?"

"I thought we weren't going to talk shop tonight."

Drawing a glass of Merlot to his lips, "No, no. Not what story you're reporting on—I mean what is *your* story."

"Me, personally?" she said, touching her chest. "Basically, it's a testament to dedication, naivete, stubbornness—the cocktail for disenchantment and ruin."

There was a long, uncomfortable silence. "Go on. I'm listening."

"You've said that there's nothing more to you than your work. What makes you think that there's anything more to me than my story?"

"You say I'm seeing my wife when I look at you. Maybe you're right."

She slowly lowered a forkful of rare filet to her plate and gazed at him. "Told you."

"But if you insist that I *know* that I'm looking at Helen Morgan, I have to know something *about* Helen Morgan." He touched her hand. His pulse quickened.

Helen withdrew her hand, opened her eyes wide, then, squinting, looked up and around. "Excuse me." She opened her handbag, withdrew a tiny fluid-filled vial, held it over her upturned head, and released two drops into each eye. She blinked, then turned to Kevin with glistening eyes. "Contacts. The dry air here plays havoc with them."

Kevin stared at her as if calculating different approaches for his next move. "Let's start with an easy question. Where are you from?"

"Everywhere. Nowhere. My father worked for the government. We moved around a lot. Before college my life was a series of two-year stints at research stations from Anchorage to Atlanta. By the time I was ten I'd learned to stop making friends."

"Until college."

"I was a broadcast-journalism major at NYU. Minored in theater." She hesitated. "For the first time my life was stable.

You can't appreciate how wonderful it is to wake up in the morning and know that you'll be in the same place, and that the people you meet and care about will still be there, too." She pushed a slice of meat across her plate. "I was exactly where I wanted to be: New York. I was going to be a network anchor."

"You certainly have the drive and the intelligence. And," gently smiling, "you wouldn't look bad in front of the camera, either."

"That dream died when my father did."

"I'm sorry. Money problems?"

Her fingers stiffened. "Among other things."

"It must have been difficult. But you're still in the business. Don't count yourself out."

She looked away from him—in part, a strategic move, but in part because it was difficult to face him. "I wound up interning at KIFI-TV in southern Idaho. It didn't work out, but I managed to get a job at the *Idaho Falls Post Register.* Which has led me to this increasingly pleasant dinner."

He raised his glass to her. She speared her filet.

From within the safe confines of her limousine's tinted rear window, Joan Tetlow, hands rigidly clasped, stared at the entrance to Le Bec-Fin. A man carrying a box dodged across Walnut Street, slid between parked cars, and rapped on the limousine's rear window. Her driver released the lock. The man jumped into the seat beside her.

Carefully, he opened the box. It contained bubble sheets wrapped around a sealed jar with crumbs and a water goblet. "Will this do?"

A sixtyish woman with tight silvery hair, teardrop diamond earrings, and husband-on-arm approached Kevin. "Dr. Kincaid? We saw you on TV. We wanted to tell you that what you're doing is wonderful. Years ago, we," glancing at her man, "lost a child to cystic fibrosis. No one should ever have to go through that." Her smile evaporated. "No one."

Helen studied Kevin as the couple moved on. She knew she had to maneuver ever more carefully. "Enjoy being in the spotlight?"

"You're the reporter. That's where *you* want to wind up."

"I'll take that as a yes."

"Then you'd be wrong. The only reason I ventured in was to dismantle the legal roadblocks hampering my work." He sat back. "I have absolutely no desire to see my private life, such as it is, plastered on tabloids by the checkout aisles."

She sighed. "You, Dr. Kincaid, are afraid of opening up to anyone. Especially me."

He tossed his napkin on the table. "Bullshit. You've seen me with Donny."

"That's hardly revealing. I could've been watching that commercial—excuse me, public service announcement—tonight on TV."

"You still haven't explained how you knew the content of the Association's PSA *before* it was aired. That was a closely guarded secret. Only a few senior officials at the Association and the network knew what was being aired. Now if—" Kevin stopped speaking. He appeared to be listening to a delicate classical piece being played in the background. After a handful of notes, he called the maître d' over and slipped him $100. "Please change the music. Something less—airy."

The maître d' looked perplexed. "Sir?"

Kevin slipped him another $100. "I don't care what. Just as long as there's no flute."

The man shrugged and left. Thirty seconds later, a neutral Bach piece played.

"Why did you do that?" Helen asked.

"How did you know about the commercial?" Kevin shot back.

"Trade you. Even up."

Kevin crossed his arms.

"Oh, all right! My editor may run a small-town newspaper, but more than a few network execs have started out in the boonies."

"Somehow I don't think that's the whole truth."

"Impugning my word is a poor defense for going back on yours."

"Okay, okay. At the funeral, my sister-in-law insisted on a flutist. The damn bastard played 'Amazing Grace.' It seems like I hear it all the time, but it's especially bad when I hear a flute solo. Changing background music is easy. But there're times when I have to be a bit more resourceful to drown out the sounds."

"Such as?"

"I studied Kung Fu a few years, as if I could learn to parry and punch the pain. But the only thing that ever helped silence that god-awful flute was work." He poured himself another glass. "And running. Endorphins, for a short time, purge my mind."

"Purge it for what?"

"Work," he said.

"Catatonia may seem a blessing, but you miss the highs, as well as the lows."

"I've had my share of both the last two days. Personally and professionally."

Could he be having doubts about his employers? Helen reached for the CD in her purse, then decided not to pursue it. "Kevin, when was the last time you felt exhilarated?"

He smiled. "Are you asking when the last time I was in bed with a woman?"

"Down, boy. I mean, when was the last time you felt—free?"

He leaned back, stared up at the chandelier. "I was standing on an old railroad trestle over the Perkiomen River, maybe eighty feet above the water. We were camping for the day, and some kids had dared me. I stood on the edge, looked down at that brown water—and I jumped." Slowly, a grin emerged. "There's this embracing, electrifying, terrifying delight. Your mind tricks you, tells you that your feet are just about to touch the ground the next instant. The next. Then the next. With each lie, you become more alive."

"How'd it feel when you hit the water?"

"I struck the river, legs stiff, but angled a bit forward. It wasn't a hard smack, I just kind of slid in and shot down, but at an angle that redirected the force of the fall to drive me back to the surface. I remember opening my eyes. The river was so murky, I couldn't see my hand in front of my face. I fought my way up, hands groping for the surface. I held my breath, using the same mind trick, promising myself that the surface was just an instant away."

"Boys! How old were you?"

"Eight. I remember because it was the last time before—" He stopped.

If only I can get him to open up. She stroked the back of his hand. "I'm listening."

"My father worked late, sometimes seven nights a week. He'd had an affair shortly after I was born. That ended, but my mother never fully trusted him again. She'd regularly greet him at the door with accusations. And before you ask whether she was right, the answer is—who knows? But this," holding up and swirling a glass of wine, "was her solution." He finished the glass. "Then Donny came and things really went wrong."

"How so?"

"Donny was 'unexpected.' Halfway through her pregnancy my mother knew that she was carrying a child with Down syndrome. When he was born he also had severe neurologic problems, which the doctors promptly attributed to her drinking. My father blamed my mother. My mother blamed herself. And me, I blamed Donny."

"Why?"

"My family may have been dysfunctional, but at least it was a family. Donny shattered that." He shrugged. "One morning I tried to wake up my mother. Her arms were cold." His jaw muscles flexed. "You know, people really can will themselves to die."

Helen's fingers caressed his hand. She blinked rapidly. "I've ruined your evening."

The waiter presented him with the bill. Kevin placed a platinum credit card in the book and handed it back without looking. "Remember Wendy? The woman you met at the hospital? Well, over the years, she's seen many pictures of my wife. Know what she whispered in my ear?"

Helen blew her nose. Shook her head.

" 'Second chances come only once.' "

Helen Morgan returned his gaze. "Take me back to my hotel," she rasped. "I've something to share with you."

Tetlow's fingernails digging into the seat, "Move your people into position. We may only have this one chance."

The man in the front seat relayed her orders. A moment later he said, "Don't worry, Ms. Tetlow. My people have all the angles covered."

Kevin and Helen appeared at the restaurant's front entrance. Kevin signaled the valet to bring the car.

"I don't see any of your men. Where are your men?" Tetlow snapped.

The valet helped Helen into the car. Kevin tipped the man and drove off.

"Did they get it? Did they get it?"

A man in a short leather jacket hurried across the street, walked up to Tetlow's car, and handed a disk to the man in front. "Here they are, Ms. Tetlow," he said, "your photos."

Adam's Mark Hotel
Philadelphia   *10:01 P.M.*

Helen entered her hotel room with Kevin close behind her. Her dress swishing, she took his coat and hung it in her closet. "That was a wonderful dinner."

"Glad you liked it."

She approached him, her eyes just above his shoulder level. She ran a finger up and down the outside of his firm upper arm. His warm breath glided over her hair, down her back. The beat from his pounding heart jumped the narrowing gulf between them, burrowed into her chest. Eyelids drooping, she gazed up into his face, brushed back an errant lock of his hair, then touched tiny beads of perspiration on his forehead. *I must divorce mission from passion*, she thought, taking his hand, leading him into the bedroom. Placing her hands beneath his jacket, she pushed it up over his shoulders and onto the floor, then slithered her third finger beneath his collar and loosened his tie. "Let me share something precious with you," she said. "Close your eyes."

Kevin's eyes fluttered shut.

Helen pulled back. So tall, strong, tight. Yet quivering. From anticipation? Fear? She had to know whether payment should be made in advance. She took her handbag from the floor, and exposed the precious CD inside. *I have to be certain.* "Tonight, I can be your—"

"No. Don't say it. I," stifling a laugh-cry, "want *you*, Helen Morgan."

She, too, hushed a cry, closed her handbag, and gently kicked it away.

He opened his eyes, touched her chin, and raised her face to his.

She reached back, unzipped her dress, let it slink onto the floor, and stood, her body open. Errant strands of her long hair flowed over breasts billowing from her satiny chemise. "Show me."

"It's been so—such a long, long time."

For us both.

He followed her lead, undressing to taut, baby blue briefs stretched to bursting limits.

She massaged her palms in sweeping, circular motions across the tops of sparse hairs on his muscular chest. Each chest hair stiffened, aroused in synchrony to his thumping heart as she blew a stream of warm, steamy breath over them. She removed her panty hose. Let her slip fall.

He removed his briefs, released a long, shuddering breath, and trembled.

Extending her arm, she took his hand, led him to the side of the bed, and directed him to sit near the edge. She sat between his legs, her back to his chest, and brought his arms around her midriff. "Hold me." His chest warmed her chilled back. His hot breath, his desire to please her, heated her in places she thought long dead. Tucked against her back, his burning stiffness grew hotter, thicker. Stronger.

She turned her face to him. Their lips met, at first, closed. She widened hers, and felt his tongue gently trace their inner lining. Then pull back, waiting. She gave a long, lingering glance at the strong man who wanted to please her, and responded in kind. Their mouths spread in unison, their tongues meeting, exploring, playfully dancing around each other, entwining, battling to be with and within the other. She guided his hands across her abdomen. Up and beneath her breasts. He held them in adulation, as if they were precious, fragile treasures. Adoring fingertips glided up over their curves, pausing gently over her nipples before they touched in ever-tightening circles. The burning engorgement in her back grew hotter. Wanting more. It was time.

Her right hand caressed his. She led it away from her breasts—down across her belly, her pelvis, along her right thigh, and inward. She released his hand. It skipped to the other thigh, slowly slid inward, and again skipped the sensuous center. His fingers glided back and forth between her legs, each pass denying the touch to desirous flesh that needed, screamed for it. She could not wait.

As if hearing her body's screams, his fingers touched her tender flesh. Stroked it gently. It was already wet, sticky with excitement. Slowly up, slowly down. Her body swayed to each stroke. His strokes increased in strength, in speed, in intensity to her desire. More, she wanted. More.

He followed the changing rhythms of her body. Her skin gleamed with sweat. Her tongue no longer able to dance, her mouth needed to be open, to moan. She needed his rhythmic strokes higher, to touch her incarnation of ecstasy. He could not know; she had to show him.

But his hand moved, so slightly up and in. To her place of purest pleasure.

"Ohhh!" She felt him stroke her anew, following the movements of her body, whispering in her ear of her beauty, of delicious promises, of unquestioned, unrestrained fulfillment of her most hidden desires. She grimaced with pleasure, feeling him grow beside her as her body rocked, holding back for that one lost moment before absolute ecstasy. One last second.

Her body erupted. She convulsed in rapture.

His arms tightened around her middle as her body writhed from aftershocks. He kissed her cheek, her neck, her shoulder, and hugged her again. Her ecstatic tremors slowly, slowly receded, though they burned as strong.

He started again.

As his fingers tenderly caressed between her legs, she knew it would again be wonderful. But she needed to transcend that level. She brought her hand around to his face and lightly kissed his lips. "Come, face me."

He picked up his leg and swiveled around to face her, his fingers continuing ever-heightening strokes. She touched his shoulder. He folded, kneeling before her.

She whispered, "If you'd rather not—"

"Shhh!" He kissed her knee, touched his tongue to her thigh, and drew a long, wet curve inward. He lifted his head, and began again. First one leg, then the other, then back. Never coming home.

Her fervor rose. What was he waiting for?

He touched his tongue to her most tender spot. She wriggled as wave upon wave of electricity surged through her. He changed his rhythm to match the slowly strengthening beats of her body. She whined in expectation. He suddenly stopped.

"Please," she panted. "Please!"

He touched the barest tip of his tongue to where she cried out.

She erupted. Stronger, so much stronger than before. And deeper. But not deep enough.

She motioned him onto the bed. He scrambled to her. They sat facing each other, legs spread wide. They gazed a moment into each other's eyes, then she shimmied between his legs, his thighs. Drenched in perspiration, her skin tingled from waves of heat that arose from the tip of his erectness. Closer, she moved. It touched her. She quaked with anticipation. They leaned into each other, kissing wildly, devouring each other. She grabbed his fullness, growing in girth, and hot, scorching hot. Its swelled underside pulsating, she felt his heart beat in her palm.

His lips broke away. He reached out and caressed her cheek. Helen gazed at him. He was not looking on her as conquest, but with empathy, with genuine desire to fulfill her. She knew he would be happy to bask in whatever warmth she would give back.

Half lunging forward, she guided him inside. She rocked as his burning filled her, the bed thumping to the ferocity of their rhythm. Deeper, expanding, he filled her. Overfilled her. His pulse pounded within her, joining his heart to hers. Her insides, permeated with pleasure. More—she wailed to his driving, thrusting expansion—more. More! She had to have him!

He furiously convulsed within her. She exploded with euphoria. He convulsed again. Her body responded in spectacular kind. He rumbled again inside her, a mini-burst of exhilaration.

The powerful fullness within her slowly deflated, retreated. His matted chest hairs pressed against her as she tried to squeeze out the last drops of his fullness. He raised her chin and softly touched his lips to hers. Skin tingling, pelvis reverberating with ghostly echoes of his rhythm, her mind lazily swam through a choking ecstasy.

Never before had she—never before. "Were you making love to me or your wife?"

Stupid! she thought. *Stupid! Why did you do that? He'll—*

". . . was you. *You* were the one who brought me back."

She still felt his heat inside her, strong as ever. Out of the corner of her eye, she saw her handbag strap protruding from beneath the bed. There'd be plenty of time in the morning to show him the Program. It could wait.

DARPA (Defense Advanced Research Projects Agency)
Director's Office, S&I (Security & Intelligence)
Arlington, Virginia

Kristin Brocks took off her reading glasses and dully stared at the small holographic-image projector on her desktop. She'd already played the Collaborate's last intercepted communication twenty-five times, hoping to discover some hidden nuance she'd missed. On her 26th playing, she focused on the image of the silhouette. The apparition said: "I'll consult our contacts within DARPA."

After two years of investigations with surveillance satellites, hidden operatives, and planning, they'd finally said openly what she'd feared all along: the Agency had been compromised. But the intercepted communication told her more: the Collaborate was going to ground. Thinking back, her meeting on the ski lift had been a mistake. Loring's carefully crafted comments about her divorce had caught her off guard and neutralized her edge. And she'd compounded that blunder with an ill-conceived closing bravado. Brocks chided herself for allowing her shattered feelings to disrupt the focus of her life.

Her computer beeped and displayed a tiny phone icon in the center of her screen: it was an incoming call. Immediately, she downloaded the holographic message onto one of the Agency's ultra-high-density transparent data crystals, pocketed it, deleted and destroyed the parent file on the network, then put the call through. A man appeared on her monitor: Dr. Quentin Hicks, Director of the Defense Sciences Office. DSO was DARPA's largest technical office and its technological conscience, charged with developing the most promising arenas of basic science and engineering research and bringing them into the Defense Department. DSO generally handled cryogenics, holographic data storage systems, virtual integrated prototyping modeling, and biomimetic systems—but there were notable exceptions. The DSO Director, though not her superior, required some measure of deference. "Good evening, Dr. Hicks. You're up late."

"They wouldn't listen to you?" Hicks asked.

"Loring laughed in my face."

"Why are they being so unreasonable?"

"Because they can."

Hicks wiped his sweaty forehead. "One of my sources verified that Kincaid has, indeed, produced a vector capable of transporting full sets of artificial chromosomes in animal cells with one hundred percent transfection efficacy and one hundred percent specificity. We want it. We're entitled to it under the terms of the collaboration."

"They don't see it that way. Their agreement with us was dissolved years before Kincaid perfected his vector. Even before our tête-à-tête, Loring facetiously invited me to bring it up in open court."

Hicks rapped his index finger on the table. "Who cares what they think? I just want to know how *you* are going to get it!"

She tried to rub the exhaustion from her eyes. She didn't want to argue, but knew the next place that finger was going to point was at her. "Quentin, I've spent every waking hour of the last few years trying to clean up your mess."

"*My—*"

"You were project manager."

Dr. Hicks smiled nastily. "All this time and you still don't understand the System. This agency is dedicated to high-risk technology research free from bureaucracy. We're small, flexible, autonomous, unconstrained by conventional thinking, a bunch of freewheeling zealots pursuing unconventional goals, willing to accept failure *if* the payoff is sufficiently high. Here we develop long-term projects that require extended focus. Here we employ 'Technology Push' by identifying technologies that could make a difference, working them through to their limits and translating them into what this country will need—*tomorrow*. Now, should I repeat that, Kristin, or just put it in big, easy-to-read typeface?"

Brocks put on her reading glasses. "By all our SOPs, that Controlled Biological Systems project should have been kept *wholly within the government*. You set in motion a disaster by subcontracting to private industry, not to mention fully collaborating with them."

"That's what we do here, you overpriced security guard! We set up innovative agreements with the private sector outside of federal acquisition regulations. Projects likely to support both commercial nonmilitary and military applications. We cost-share with these companies, and then forecast what they'll do with our shared technology."

"Well, your former collaborators have used these shared resources to implement a program that not only threatens national security, but the foundation of western civilization. You made a deal with the devil." She tossed her glasses back on the desk. "And he still has plenty of silent disciples listening within this agency!"

"So, damn it, bring in the FBI! Or NSA! Or Homeland!"

"Your former friends would consider that provocative. Dr. Hicks, they have copies of the files on your special Controlled Biological System's project. If threatened they'll dump the entire contents onto a slew of websites. Need I go into the far-reaching consequences? As Project Manager your name would appear at the top of the indictment." He emphatically shook his head. "Think again," she continued. "You deliberately covered up that some of your industrial partners were not—American. On a project such as this, that's more than enough."

He buried his head in his hands. "I thought you supported the Project."

"I do. Which is why I'm keeping this matter internal and tight. So," putting on her glasses, "shall we refrain from finger-pointing?"

Adam's Mark Hotel

Beneath warm sheets in darkness pierced by the blue LCD digits of her alarm clock, Helen cooed as Kevin's hand slowly, slowly ventured toward the underside of her breasts. Her back tingled from his tender kisses moving down her spine. The phone rang. Reluctantly, she answered.

"It is Anna."

Helen brushed Kevin's roaming fingers from her chest, turned on her side, and clamped the receiver against her ear. "I have—company."

"Kincaid, yes?" Anna hesitated. "Trent knows that we copied the Program."

Helen felt Kevin's hand glide across her shoulder. She stepped from the bed. The covers fell away. "How?"

"Trent has many people hidden in many places. This is the

first chance I have had to talk to you since—" Anna's voice
cracked. "He almost killed me."

"Oh my God! What did he do?"

"Push me off my office building roof."

The bipolar bastard, she thought. "Are you okay?"

"Ja, ja. I am unhurt. He has a message for you. He says that
you may show the doctor your evidence, if we return every
copy to him later."

"I don't understand his about-face."

"Nor I. But Trent said that your time is running out."

Helen smiled reassuringly at Kevin. "Not a problem."

"He is in bed with you?"

"Oh, yes," she rasped.

"He—pleased you?"

Helen turned away from Kevin. "You're a good friend, but
that's none of—"

"You have been trained to confuse him. Do not become confused yourself."

Covering her mouth, whispering into the phone, "He wants
me."

"Helen—Kevin Kincaid is going to die."

The room began spinning. She felt light-headed, suddenly cold.

"Trent intends to kill him by Friday."

Helen's right contact felt dry. "Maybe you're wrong."

"Perhaps. But if you have not convinced Kincaid to join us
by then, Trent certainly will."

Her eye started to burn. She rubbed harder. "Talk to you
later." And hung up the phone.

"Who was that?" Kevin asked.

"One of my sources," she said, blinking against her contact
lens.

Kevin tossed off the sheets. Nude, partially erect, he turned
to her. "You're trembling." He touched the hand over her
mouth. "What is it? Are you in trouble?"

Massaging her pained eye, she nodded.

"Helen, let me help." He held her arms.

Her irritated eye suddenly felt better. "Oh, no!"

"What? What?"

"My contact just popped out." She dropped to the floor and began scouring for it with extended fingers. "Don't move."

"I'll get the light."

"No!" She continued groping in the dark.

"Helen, this is silly. Let's turn on a lamp."

"Kevin, don't—"

He flicked on the nightstand light—and caught a full view of her face. One eye was green, the other pure, intense blue. His look turned pained, as if he'd just been struck.

"I've, uh, I've always worn colored contacts," she whispered. "I love green."

He recoiled from her. "My Helen's eyes were gray-green. Not something you'd find on the shelf. Those lenses had to be custom-made."

"Kevin, let me ex—"

"Your resemblance to my Helen was no accident! You made yourself up to look like her. Talk like her. My God, you even had her mannerisms, her likes, her—You used me—used me to get close enough to steal V_7."

"It wasn't that at all. You don't under—"

"Who's behind it? Radical extremists? Fundamentalists? Some greedy CEO?

"Kevin, please—"

"Shut up!" He gathered his tousled clothes. "Was it fun playing dress-up? Playing on my loneliness—my longing for the only woman I ever loved?" He slapped on his shirt, pants, shoes. "Tell me, what did they pay you to hurt me like this?" His eyes watery, "What the hell kind of person are you, that you could do this?" The door slammed behind him.

Helen staggered to the bathroom and looked in the wide mirror. The face that stared back had one blue and one gray-green eye. Half Helen Morgan, half Helen Kincaid. She was a nothing, a nobody, an amalgam of dreams: her own submerged nightmare and Kevin Kincaid's fantasy. She collapsed onto the tiles and curled up, her knees to her chest. She'd failed for her father, for her brother, for herself, and for the rest of humanity.

ACGD Commercial #3—
"Germline Gene Therapy: What Might My Brother Have Achieved?"

The following commercial aired on all major broadcast and cable networks the evening of Tuesday, January 21 and late night/early morning Wednesday, January 22:

[VIDEO]:   *Opening shot of Dr. Kevin Kincaid.*

DR. KEVIN KINCAID: I'm Dr. Kevin Kincaid. For the past few nights, you've kindly let me into your homes to tell you about the promise of germline gene therapy. You've let me tell you how, one day, germline gene therapy may not only prevent genetic diseases in our children, but actually eliminate such diseases from the face of the earth. Now, let me give you a very personal reason.

[VIDEO]:   *Camera pans back.*

KINCAID: My brother, Donny.

[VIDEO]   *Camera reveals Kincaid standing beside his brother, Donnelly Kincaid, in a wheelchair in a home.*

KINCAID: A hundred years ago, people would have called Donny a "mongoloid idiot." Today, we know his condition as Down syndrome, or Trisomy 21. Now, in many cases, people with Down syndrome can lead nearly normal lives. A few, like my Donny, are not so lucky. Donny also has other genetic disabilities.

[VIDEO]:   *Camera pushes in for close-up of Donnelly.*

KINCAID: Normal cells have twenty-three pairs of chromosomes.

> [VIDEO]:   *CGI (Computer-Generated Imaging) Animation: Graphic of a human cell with twenty-three pairs of squiggly white strings (chromosomes) in the center (nucleus).*

KINCAID (OFF-CAMERA VOICEOVER [VO]): Unfortunately, Donny's cells have an extra chromosome number 21.

> [VIDEO]:   *CGI Animation: Appearance of an additional red squiggly string (chromosome) beside one of the chromosome pairs. Close-up of the chromosome triplet: one red intertwined with two white.*

KINCAID (VO): The only way we can ever hope to cure his genetic disease would be with gene therapy.

> [VIDEO]:   *CGI Animation: The red chromosome breaks apart and disappears.*

KINCAID (VO): But it's too late for Donny.

> [VIDEO]:   *Transition to close-up of Donnelly.*

KINCAID (VO): Even if we knew how to get rid of the extra chromosome that causes his genetic disability, we could never change all of the many billions of cells in his body. We needed to cure him *before* he was born. He needed germline gene therapy.

> [VIDEO]:   *Transition to CGI Animated Sequence: View of cell and center of cell (nucleus). Zoom in on center of cell, with crumpled white strings (the chromosomes) and one black, misshapen string (deformed chromosome.)*

KINCAID (VO): In the center of every cell in our body is a nucleus. This nucleus contains strands of DNA, called chromosomes. Each chromosome contains hundreds or thousands of genes made of DNA. These genes are the blueprints for our bodies. But sometimes, something goes terribly wrong.

[VIDEO]:   *Animated Sequence: Focuses in on misshapen black string.*

KINCAID (VO): Just a few wrong DNA molecules on one gene of one chromosome can mean a lifetime of suffering.

[VIDEO]:   *Split screen. Animated Sequence on left. Montage of sick children on right.*

KINCAID (VO): Down syndrome. Cystic fibrosis. Sickle cell. Tay-Sachs. Beta-thalassemia. The list goes on. No matter what medicines we give these children, we'll never fix their genes. Their disability will be carried on, generation after generation after generation. Unless . . .

[VIDEO]:   *Full-screen CGI Animation: A bubble-enclosed white string (new chromosome) enters the cell and penetrates the nucleus. The white chromosome replaces the mis-shapen, black chromosome in the cell.*

KINCAID (VO): Unless we get rid of those disease-causing genes in every cell and replace them with healthy, working genes *before* there are too many cells to fix.

[VIDEO]:   *CGI Animation: Pan back. See many cells with de-formed, black chromosomes replaced by healthy white chromosomes. Then hundreds of cells. Then the outline of an arm. Then the outline of a recognizably human fe-tus. The fetus morphs into a young man resembling an idealized version of Donnelly Kincaid, without the phys-ical characteristics of Down syndrome.*

KINCAID (VO): It's called germline gene therapy. And it might have prevented what happened to my brother.

[VIDEO]:   *Dissolve to Donnelly's actual facial appearance. Camera pans back to Kincaid standing beside him.*

KINCAID (ON CAMERA): I love my brother. He's special. I wouldn't trade him for the world. But, sometimes, I wonder what he might have achieved if he had been given the same chance in life as me. Maybe you know someone like that, too.

[VIDEO]:   *Freeze-frame of Donnelly.*

KINCAID: Call your senators! Demand their support for House Bill 601. Lift the ban on germline gene therapy. Tell them to vote *for* House Bill 601! Give our children a chance!

[VIDEO]:   *End Tag: Add supered letters to lower third of screen.*
SUPPORT HOUSE BILL 601!
GIVE OUR CHILDREN A CHANCE![SM]
Paid for by the Association to Cure Genetic Disabilities.
Hold image for five seconds. Fade to black.

5

Marguerite Moraes pressed her face against the OR theater's plastic dome. Far below, the emergency team worked furiously, fighting the ventricular tachycardia that had turned the little boy's heart into a bag of wriggling worms. Marguerite wiped away her tears. So much potential wasted. She wanted to beg God to at least let Ethan taste life, but obviously, He had scorned them all.

Delphi had no graveyard. What would they do with the boy afterward? After Ethan, only one child remained. When the last one went—she tried not to think of what would happen to her.

A short man with bulging forearms and wearing surgical blues approached her. He said, "We've stabilized the boy."

"What now, Doctor?"

"We've tried everything. His seizures have progressed from partial type, located in discrete areas of the cerebral cortex, to severe, generalized, tonic-clonic type, spreading across his higher centers. We've titrated him with front-line therapies, then adjunctive and second-lines. We've tried drugs in four experimental families in addition to a unique formulation synthesized by Dr. Ambrose downstairs. Nothing's worked. The child is progressing through to status epilepticus. The seizures will begin lasting longer than thirty minutes, piling up on each other without time for recovery. Before long, standard therapy for status epilepticus will fail. It might be weeks or days, perhaps only hours." He folded his arms. "You've been through this before."

"Can't you do *anything?*"

"The autopsy may tell us why he survived longer than the others."

"Might it help Meredith? She's the last survivor, you know."

"I've said too much already. We'll inform you when the boy's status changes." The doctor spun on his sneakers and left.

He knows what's killing them! she thought. *I'm going to get Meredith out of here before they kill her, too!*

Adam's Mark Hotel

The face in the mirror that stared back at Helen Morgan was a hybrid of her shattered self. She'd thrown away the gray-green contacts, leaving her with her natural, blue eyes. Her cheeks had returned to their sallow shade, but her hair was now dyed obsidian black. For her own safety she could never allow her hair to return to its natural blond color. She turned off the bathroom light. Her half-packed suitcases lay strewn across the bed and couch, but she had nowhere to go.

The red light on her telephone blinked: a message, probably from Trent, or his sniveling sycophant, Straub. She phoned the front desk.

"Package for you, Ms. Morgan," the clerk said.

"Who from?"

"There's no return address. Should I have it sent up?"

"Yes, please." Then she hung up. *What's in the package? Who sent it? Trent? No, unmarked packages aren't his style. Kevin? Not likely, after the look in his eyes. Who else knows where I am?*

Helen answered the knock at her door. A messenger stood holding a sealed brown, bubble-lined envelope. She absently handed him $10 then closed the door in his face.

The package was dirty and mail-worn. She cradled it, back-side up. A mail bomb? She held her breath and flipped it over. It was addressed to Helen Morgan, care of the Adam's Mark Hotel. And written in familiar block lettering. She dropped to her knees, ripped open the package, and spilled out the contents: a note, dated January 20; a mini audiocassette; a camcorder-sized videocassette; and two vials with spongy, pinkish-white tissue suspended in clear liquid. She seized the letter and began reading:

> *Tracy,*
>
> *I found the Collaborate installation. It's on Tiburon Island, Mexico. I've been inside. You can't imagine what they've done to the Seris! I almost broke down. I've caught it on audio and video. The world's got to see this. But the Collaborate's so powerful and people are so cynical that I'm afraid this will be dismissed along with UFO sightings and alien autopsies. So I included two specimens. They're tissue samples from a little girl they mutilated. Take it to someone you trust. Have them do a full work-up. Make sure they do a 'KARYOTYPING.' It may be our only proof. You can fake pictures and sounds, but you can't fake DNA.*
>
> *Tracy, whatever you do, KEEP THIS AWAY FROM TRENT! I'll try to meet up with you in Philly or D.C. If I don't show up in the next week, try looking at the old place in Virginia. But, whatever happens, promise me that you won't come after me! Because if I'm not there, I'm probably dead. I love you, Sis.*
>
> *Always, Lance*

Helen wiped her eyes, took the videotape, inserted it in the camcorder lying on her suitcase, and opened its viewer. She began to play the tape.

BFMC, Kincaid's Office

Kevin sat in his office, his mind at war with itself. On one side intellectual centers used pure logic to predict the complex interactions of biochemical electron shells. The problem with V_7 was the stiffness of the harpoon used to penetrate and tag the cell membrane, a problem attributable to its constituent sequence of amino acids. Painstakingly, his mind plucked possible amino acids from the air and ran them through a reconstruction algorithm to see whether they would fit the growing chain that slowly was becoming a new harpoon. A charged polar amino acid here. A substituted basic amino acid for an acidic one there. A less rigid uncharged polar amide-group amino acid with a hydroxyl group replacing a more rigid amide one. Only a handful of people in the world could mentally perform so many complex chemical reactions so quickly. But the root of his brilliance, that unswervingly perfect memory, was also the source of his anguish. So often it had turned against him by flawlessly immersing him in the sights, the smells, the senses of his personal tragedies, forcing him to relive those moments again and again. Only discipline and constant work had checked the flood of memories and the pain.

The solution to V_7's problem was coming together in part of his mind—while the other part displayed a montage of blue- and gray-green-eyed Helen-faces, plastered on darkness, each image begging his forgiveness. She'd left him raw, bleeding, wanting to die. He fought harder to modify V_7, even as Helen- faces were being incorporated into the harpoon's new amino acid sequence.

BFMC, Cafeteria

Joan Tetlow shoved her spoon deep into her grapefruit, the breakfast she'd been denied because of the paper mountain that had accumulated on her desk the last few days. The grapefruit squirted her. She rubbed a burning eye clear, then glanced up. A woman with long, silky-black hair, carrying a man's overcoat, strode quickly across the lobby. *Was that her?*

BFMC, Kincaid's Office

Kevin felt the solution coming. Amino acids were dropping into the new harpoon protein sequence like the last few words filling a crossword puzzle. The new harpoon slowly transformed. Slowly, it was becoming a living, twisting, stereoscopic ribbon twisting in his mind. Soon, he'd have the harpoon's preliminary sequence. Perhaps next week his coworkers could begin synthesizing and testing.

Heated voices from outside his door touched the edges of his consciousness, like fragments of overheard conversation in a crowded mall. One was his secretary. He couldn't clearly hear the other.

There it was—his mind presenting it with perfect clarity: the fix for V_7's flaw! Kevin turned to his computer, opened the protein sequencing program, started a new file, and began entering one-letter amino acid codes:

1   MAGQLRTPKWESYLGFFEFDWQEIVGSAFEDNPPQTGVNICAYDQWSLEG 50
51 FKLKQVINSEDDNH—

A woman with long black hair and hot blue eyes burst into the office.

His eyes locked on to hers. "Helen, you've changed the face that launched a thousand ships. So who do those blue eyes belong to?"

"They're mine."

"The black hair, too?"

She folded his overcoat and laid it on a chair.

"Thanks for returning it. Now that that's done," voice trembling, "so are we."

"Kevin, you're a brilliant, sensitive man. But sometimes you're so myopic, so naive that—"

"So now it's my fault?"

"I risked my life coming here to save yours."

"No more cloak-and-dagger!" Pointing, "Door's unlocked."

She glanced at the monitor and VCR on a cart in the corner, then opened her handbag and withdrew a videocassette. "Here's the Ghost of Christmas Future." She turned on the monitor and VCR and put the tape in the slot. Shaky images, seemingly from a jostled handheld camera, appeared on the TV of a somber, granite-block building rising out of marshland enclosed by a high, barbed-wire fence. The image jumped to out-of-focus figures, children, moving around the compound. Not clustered together, playing, but walking erratically. "This is Isla de Tiburon, Mexico."

"Camera work's not very good," he said.

"The cameraman may be dead."

The picture zoomed in on three children. One child had distorted neck muscles that twisted his head three-quarters backward. Another had massively enlarged chest muscles on the right side, with atrophied muscles on the left side. A third, swollen legs like tree stumps. Each hobbled.

"I've never seen such a collection of neuromuscular asymmetries. Did you get this from the island of Tiburon or *The Island of Doctor Moreau*?"

The picture jumped to a tiled lab with old equipment: biological safety cabinets, orbital shakers, cell-culture incubators, low-power microscopes. Seemingly shot from an exterior window, the picture panned to a back room, then zoomed in. Two men in white coats knelt alongside a dark-skinned little girl in chains. Her head bulged on its left side, hideously distorting her face like a cut-away diagram in an anatomical atlas. Her left shoulder was bloated, covered with oozing ulcers, and dislocated high on her collarbone. The other shoulder was withered, frail. Her left arm, manacled, rattled inch-thick chain links as she squirmed in terror. One man produced a scalpel and approached the toddler while his partner applied a tourniquet to her arm. He began carving through skin to burgeoning biceps beneath. The little girl screamed.

"My God! What's he doing?" Kevin exclaimed, her wails vibrating through his chest. "He's not even using anesthesia! What kind of doctor—"

"One without conscience, testing the muscular strength of his 'experiment' under duress. That's all these children were to those monsters—just guinea pigs."

The man dissected deeper. He isolated a chunk of ultra-dense pink flesh with a pair of pick-ups and plopped it into a fluid-filled vial. Helen froze the tape.

Kevin turned away from the vivisection. "It's a hoax."

"You know it wasn't." Helen shut her eyes. "It gets worse."

"Why are you showing me this?"

"These deformities didn't occur naturally. They were induced."

"Induced? By what? Some kind of radiation?"

"You just don't see it."

"See what?"

Shaking her head, "What your vector can do."

"Oh, no! No way! I'm not responsible for that!"

Helen knelt beside him. Touched his hand. "Oh, but my sweet Kevin, you *are!*"

Loring's Estate
Berks County, Pennsylvania

Loring poured himself a drink from the bar, then seated himself opposite the bolted doors. It had been two years since he'd spent an evening at his Berks County estate. The library, similar to but larger than the one in Santa Fe, afforded a view of his private golf course nestled in rich farmland between rural Lancaster and urban Delaware valleys. Though maintained by a skeleton staff, the house had a faint, musty odor—an odor that had to be removed before evening.

"Thirty seconds to incoming transmission," announced the synthetic voice.

Unlike yesterday's private holographic conference with Bertram, this would be a Quorum Summit, with at least seven of the principal seventeen members participating, though all were rarely in the same hemisphere, let alone the same country. Aside from Bertram, the participants varied from meeting to meeting. Quorum Summits yielded to the chemistry of their participants: sometimes afternoon tea, often trench warfare.

Red, blue, green lights scanned him. In the background, a faint A-minor chord chimed. In the far corner of the room, the pseudo-image rotund silhouette appeared at a desk: Bertram.

Five other holographic images appeared in the room: Floyd Elliston, dressed in jeans and cutting a steak; Andrea Beller, in a black *tobok* in the middle of a Taiji pattern; Euan McDonald, feet propped on a couch and smoking a pipe; Stuart Knorr, slumped in a chair, hand propping up a sleepy head; and Wolfgang Vorpahl, in an impeccably tailored suit, and sitting at attention. The Americans and the Australian were principals in biotech industries; the German brought vast holdings in communications and banking to the table. In the Collaborate's early, formative years, many members had pushed to include representatives from the Middle East and North Africa, citing their potentially enormous financial assets. Bertram had steadfastly refused to allow a citizen of any Muslim state to join—which particularly puzzled the membership, considering Bertram's extensive travels throughout Asia and Africa. The Collaborate had nearly disbanded over the issue. Then came the atrocities in New York. After that, no one ever questioned his decisions.

"We have a Quorum," the Bertram silhouette began. "First on the agenda: Tiburon. As you all know, the facility had to be dismantled due to a security breach. There was insufficient time to call for a referendum."

"Breached by who? The government?" Floyd Elliston asked between bites of beef.

"You've all received, by courier, Mr. Loring's report on the meeting with the DARPA security chief," Bertram said. "They knew about Tiburon, but kept their distance."

"Doesn't answer my question," Elliston said.

Bertram answered, "The matter is under investigation."

"Estimated loss in U.S. dollars?" Wolfgang Vorpahl asked quietly.

"The facility was antiquated," Bertram said. "The final tally, allowing for discounting, less than $150 million American, excluding graft to Mexican officials. Sustainable."

"Total loss, ya mean," Elliston spat, slamming down his fork. "What the hell did we get out of that place anyway?"

"Data, Mr. Elliston," Bertram said slowly, emphatically. "We know that the new genes synthesized for musculoskeletal structure are fully effective. Don't we?"

"Yeah."

"And we know that the chromosome carrying them can, in theory, be fully inserted into human cells. Don't we, Mr. Elliston?"

"Yeah."

"And we know, from autopsies of female subjects, that induced genetic alterations are present in subjects' egg cells and are, therefore, carried into the germline and passed from generation to generation. That was our intent, was it not, Mr. Elliston?"

"Uh-huh."

"And through creative cost sharing, the bulk of funds for establishing Tiburon came, unwittingly, through DARPA. Did it not?"

"I know, I know."

"Then certainly you must agree that Tiburon has proven itself cost-effective."

Loring smiled at the beauty of Bertram's signature sales tactics: little yes's leading the buyer into a final acceptance.

"With the final component, facilities like Tiburon and Delphi will take on lesser importance. Beta testing, primarily," Bertram said. "Item closed. Which brings us to the next order of business. The new vector, Mr. Loring?"

Loring finished his drink. "Kincaid has virtually completed formulating and testing the new vector. I hope—anticipate—presenting it to this body within two weeks."

"What about the woman at the news conference?" Andrea Beller asked, then snapped out her right hand as if delivering a punch. "Who is she?"

"The matter is being investigated."

"Why doesn't that comfort me?" Beller sneered.

Loring stared at his empty glass. "We have photographs, fingerprints, DNA samples. We're running her through every database on Earth."

"The woman knew about K_4."

"We're investigating possible leaks from Kincaid's lab and other sources."

"Like what?"

Loring put down the glass and glared at Beller's holographic image. "Like this virtual room."

The others shouted protests and accusations. Bertram banged a gavel.

"The Feds're involved," Elliston voiced.

"They're breast-beating," Loring said.

"Dixon, could there be a connection between Tiburon and that woman?" Euan McDonald asked, smoke wafting from his pipe.

Loring looked to the silhouette of Bertram. "Possibly."

"I realize that it is the policy of this organization *not* to employ extreme force against the outside world, as any such use presents a substantial risk to the Plan. Nonetheless, I believe this Quorum should grant Mr. Loring the authority to use such force as required," Bertram said. "The Chair votes yes on this matter. And the rest of this Quorum?"

The five others raised their hands.

"It's passed. Mr. Loring, I trust you'll use *discretionary* force."

Loring nodded graciously. His assignment offered a rare opportunity.

"Third order of business," Bertram resumed. "Progress on passage of U.S. House of Representatives Bill 601. Some of you have concerns regarding the handling of this matter, Herr Vorpahl."

Vorpahl adjusted his collar. "I understand the importance of this legislation. America is unrestricted by social and political restraints in European Union. Developments in United States lead to perceived inadequacies in Europe. But a $100 million bribe to a senator?"

Bertram paused. "A small sum, considering our expenditures to date, and it assures passage of Bill 601. But it will also buy other key votes that will be needed in time. In addition, I would not be surprised if much of this expenditure finds it way back into our coffers."

"*Danke.*"

"Last order of business." Bertram hesitated. "Owing to the

delicacy of progress on House Bill 601, events at Tiburon, possible security breaches, and the probability of stepped-up pressure from U.S. agencies, we will refrain from holding summits for at least a fortnight. Communications will be maintained by the courier system—with the Chair, as usual, serving as focal point."

"I don't like being left out in the cold," Elliston declared.

Bertram cleared his throat. "Let us now consider suspending all noncourier communications for the next two weeks. The Chair votes 'yes'. How does the rest of this Quorum vote?"

Loring raised his hand, as did the others, except Elliston.

Bertram whispered, "In matters of security, a unanimous vote is always less complicated."

Elliston slowly raised his hand. "I think it's a mistake to hamper free communication when we might need it most."

"So noted," Bertram said. "This session is ended. Thank you all for your time."

The holographic images disappeared.

Loring raised both fists triumphantly before smugly striding to the bar for a celebration. Seventeen years of plans and plots had culminated in an almost casual Quorum vote. *For the next two weeks, I am the Collaborate!*

BFMC

Kevin continued to stare at the blank screen after Helen removed the video. In the ten years following his residency, he'd performed more than 5,000 surgeries, cut deep into people's innards, and held living brain tissue in his hands. But to see such torture on young, horribly afflicted children. His mouth tasted vile from his churning stomach.

"You're doing better than I did," Helen said. "First time, I threw up."

"Who? Who would—"

"Your employers." She returned the tape to her handbag. "And you, Kevin."

"Me?"

"In the coffee shop, you said you'd only used vector K_4 on cell cultures."

"K_4 was a prototype. It wasn't ready for clinical trials on human beings!"

She sat on a corner of the desk and leaned in. "Apparently someone thought that it was."

"I don't believe you."

"Lance," stifling a sob, "my brother, the one who took these pictures, knew it, too." Opening her handbag, "So he sent these." She held a pair of vials with spongy, pinkish-white tissue suspended in clear liquid. "Tissue samples from one of the children. Proof that K_4 was used."

He took one of the vials. "Won't work. If HACV.K_4 was used in human germline therapy it would've been used to transfect genetic material in those children when they were embryonic, most likely while they were still little more than a blastula, a ball of cells. Any traces of K_4 would have long since been cleared."

"You told me that you abandoned K_4 because it often broke the chromosome it carried. So wouldn't that leave behind some characteristic pattern in the cells?"

Kevin reexamined the vial in his hand. "Let's see. K_4 tries to insert a new chromosome into embryonic cells. For some it succeeds, creating cells with a new extra pair of chromosomes. When those cells divide, generation by generation, they give rise to a line of cells with the new extra chromosome. For some cells it fails, inserting only fragments. In most cases those fragments aren't viable and when those cells divide, those chromosome pieces are not replicated for the next generation. For a few cells, though, it just might partially fail and—"

"Partially fail?"

"In order to be replicated when cells divide, chromosome pairs need two key segments. A centromere, that's the central portion separating the long and short arms of each chromosome. And telomeres, those are the caps at the tips of the chromosomes."

"So a few early cells had chromosome pieces with a centromere and telomere?"

"In part. So what we're left with is collections of hybrid